"Have dinner with me. Share some conversation, maybe some wine and whatever else you want,"

Reed offered. "So what do you say?"

"I say no." Jess smiled. "You must have dozens of women in a little black book somewhere, probably filed under brunettes, blondes and redheads. Why not ask one of them?"

"I don't have any redheads on the list. They've always scared me."

"Why?"

"I'll never tell."

"You can't make a statement like that and refuse to explain. What's the problem with red hair?"

He smiled wickedly. "It reminds me of fire. It's captivating and dangerous."

"But you fight fires every day."

"And so far I've never gotten burned."

Their eyes connected and suddenly the spark of fun turned into a spark of something far more serious....

Dear Reader,

It's that time of year again—pink hearts, red roses and sweet dreams abound as we celebrate that most amorous of holidays—St. Valentine's Day!

Silhouette Romance captures the sentimental mood of the month with six new tales of lovers who are meant for each other—and even if *they* don't realize it from the start, *you* will!

Last month, we launched our new FABULOUS FATHERS series with the first heartwarming tale of fatherhood. Now, we bring you the second title in the series, *Uncle Daddy*. Popular author Kasey Michaels has packed this story with humor and emotion as hero Gabe Logan learns to be a father—and a husband.

Also in February, Elizabeth August's *The Virgin Wife* whisks you away to Smytheshire, a fictional town where something dark and secret is going on. Once you've been there, you'll want to visit this wonderful, intriguing place again—and you can! Be sure to look for other Smytheshire books coming in the near future from Elizabeth August and Silhouette Romance.

To complete this month's offerings, we have book one of Laurie Paige's new ALL-AMERICAN SWEETHEARTS series, *Cara's Beloved,* as well as *To the Rescue* by Kristina Logan, *Headed for Trouble* by Joan Smith and Marie Ferrarella's *Babies on His Mind*.

In months to come, we'll be bringing you books by all your favorite authors—Diana Palmer, Annette Broadrick, Suzanne Carey and more! In the meantime, we at Silhouette Romance wish you a Happy Valentine's Day spent with someone special!

Anne Canadeo
Senior Editor

TO THE RESCUE
Kristina Logan

Silhouette
ROMANCE™
Published by Silhouette Books New York
America's Publisher of Contemporary Romance

To Dorothy and Vern,
who are always encouraging and have been known
to empty a few bookshelves in my honor.

SILHOUETTE BOOKS
300 E. 42nd St., New York, N.Y. 10017

TO THE RESCUE

Copyright © 1993 by Barbara Beharry Freethy

ISBN: 0-373-08918-X

First Silhouette Books printing February 1993

Printed in the U.S.A.

KRISTINA LOGAN

is a native Californian and a former public-relations professional who spent several exciting years working with a variety of companies whose business interests ranged from wedding consulting to professional tennis, high technology and the film industry. Now the mother of two small children, she divides her time between her family and her first love, writing.

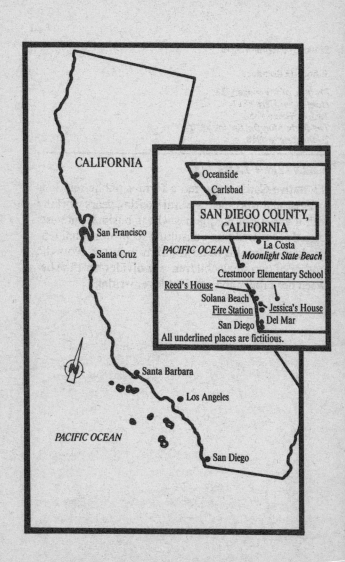

CALIFORNIA

Oceanside
Carlsbad

SAN DIEGO COUNTY, CALIFORNIA

PACIFIC OCEAN

La Costa
Moonlight State Beach

Crestmoor Elementary School

Reed's House

Solana Beach
Fire Station
San Diego

Jessica's House
Del Mar

All underlined places are fictitious.

San Francisco

Santa Cruz

Santa Barbara

Los Angeles

PACIFIC OCEAN

San Diego

Chapter One

"Come back here, you coward." Jessica Blake scrambled through the house in hot pursuit, her high heels slipping and sliding on the newly waxed hardwood floors. By the time she reached the kitchen, the only evidence of escape was a swinging screen door and a guilty look on her seven-year-old son's face. She skidded to a stop. "Andrew, you didn't."

"He didn't mean it, Mom. You scared him."

She shook her head at the pointed accusation. "He has my wallet. Now where did he go?"

"I don't know."

"Andrew..."

"In the backyard." Andrew followed her through the kitchen door. "You're not going to make him go away are you? He was just teasing you."

"Teasing?" she echoed. No, taking her wallet went beyond teasing. It was definitely malicious behavior, probably brought on by the sweltering southern California heat. Eight o'clock on a September morning, and it was already ninety-five degrees.

She had been crazy to move across the country. Nobody was the same. Just yesterday, a crowd of teenagers in a convertible had actually honked at her and called her *baby*. Baby? She was thirty years old with a son. No one in Boston would have dared to do such a thing. But Boston was miles away, and at the moment she had more pressing problems.

With a sigh, she strode over to the far end of the yard and planted her fists on her waist. "Okay, Wiley. I want my wallet. *Now.*"

The only retort was an excited bark. Jessica squatted down and peered into the doghouse. "I've got some juicy meat bones for you, just the kind you like."

Andrew peered over her shoulder. "He's not going to believe you, Mom. You never give him bones."

She threw him a disgusted look. "Do you have any better ideas?"

"Maybe if you talk to him real nice."

"Why don't you talk to him?"

"Okay." Andrew clicked his fingers together enticingly. "Come on, boy. Let's go to school."

Wiley barked in response and bolted out of the doghouse pushing Jessica over on her rear end, covering the back of her navy blue skirt in dirt. Wiley paused for a split second, sensing another disaster, and then tore off in a different direction as Jessica got up and sent him a scathing look.

"That's great. Only he didn't bring out my wallet."

"Do you want me to get it?" Andrew asked.

Jessica looked at his troubled face and shook her head. No, from here on out she was fighting her own battles, even if this one was only between her and the dog. "I'll do it. Get your backpack. We're already late for school. I never should have brought this doghouse with us. It cost a fortune to ship it across country."

"But Daddy made it for me and Wiley."

Jessica's lips tightened at the mention of her ex-husband. Theodore Blake would not have been caught dead pounding nails into boards; he was much too intellectual for manual labor. Unfortunately, Andrew didn't know that. Maybe it was time to start telling him the truth, little by little. Maybe the doghouse was a good place to start. Or... she wavered, maybe she should just get her wallet and leave the explanations for another time. Okay, so she was being a coward again. She couldn't get over all her hang-ups in one day.

"Get your things, Andrew. We'll talk about it later."

With a quick look down at her skirt, Jessica shook her head in disgust. Getting down on all fours, she poked her head into the doghouse and squinted her eyes in the dark light. She reached her hand into the interior and groped around for her wallet. She came up with nothing.

Pushing herself farther into the doghouse until both her shoulders were inside the door, she stretched out her arm, her fingers reaching the tip of the leather billfold, but it wasn't quite enough. The wood around the door to the doghouse jabbed into her side, but she took in a deep breath and squeezed forward. Her hand came around the wallet and she grabbed it triumphantly, but when she tried to back out, nothing gave. She pushed again, but the wood squeezed her body even tighter. A touch of panic went off in her mind as the darkness enveloped her.

"Andrew," she yelled. "Help me out."

Her son didn't answer, and she screamed louder. "Andrew. Where are you?"

"What's the matter?" Andrew asked breathlessly. "I was in the house getting my backpack when I heard you yell. Did you find the wallet?"

"Yes, I found the wallet. Now, I'm stuck. I need you to pull on my legs. Can you do that for me, please?"

"I guess I can try."

Jessica felt his hands grab her thighs, and he yanked, but the wood refused to give. He gamely tried again, but it was no use. "I can't do it. How did you get stuck?"

"I don't know." She rested her head on her hands as she considered the problem. "I need some help, Andrew. I have to get out of here."

"Okay, Mom. I know just what to do. They told us in school yesterday."

She heard his feet scramble around the doghouse as he took off for the house. A sudden uneasiness hit her as his words sank in. "Wait a minute. Where are you going?" No answer. "Andrew, go next door and get Mr. Gustavson." No answer. She squinted in the darkness and using her palms for leverage, she tried to push her body out of the doghouse. Her only reward was a stinging graze in her midriff where her blouse parted from her skirt. Slivers of wood stuck into her skin, and she bit back a cry of pain.

This was just what she needed. Three weeks in Solana Beach, and so far the water pipes had leaked, half her furniture had been lost somewhere in Des Moines and only a third of her kindergarten class spoke English. Now this. She had definitely hit rock bottom. Nothing else could possibly happen. Then she heard the sirens.

Loud and shrill, they blared through the still air of the suburban neighborhood, and for a split second she tried to tell herself there was a fire somewhere down the street. But the noise got louder until it finally stopped, followed by a rush of feet that made the ground tremble beneath her palms.

Then she heard a voice, low and husky and very masculine, with just enough laughter in the tone to make her blood boil.

"Mother stuck in a doghouse, just like the dispatcher said. This must be our day, Bill."

"Who's there?" Jessica called.

"Reed McAllister, Bill Carlton and Joseph Siminski, otherwise known as your local fire department."

"Can you get me out of here?"

"I sure hope so. Hey Siminski, call dispatch and tell 'em we'll be out in twenty—if we're lucky."

"What do you mean—if you're lucky?" Jessica asked warily.

His response was a chuckle deep in his throat. "Nothing for you to worry about." He paused. "Is that your mom in there, son?"

"Yes, and she's stuck," Andrew said importantly. "I called 911 just like they said in school."

Jessica groaned as she heard their conversation. She tried to wiggle out, but there was no escaping, and her cheeks began to burn as she thought of the picture she must be making with her rear end hanging out of the doghouse and her skirt hitched up around her thighs. A flush of heat swept through her body and for a second, she wished she could stay in the doghouse forever, but the touch of a hand on her thigh brought her quickly back to reality.

"What are you doing?" she demanded.

"Just checking things out, ma'am. Mind if I ask why you're in there?"

"I was looking for my wallet."

"In the doghouse?"

"Wiley brought it in here."

"Who's Wiley?"

"Our dog," Andrew interrupted. "Can you get her out?"

"Is the dog in there too?"

"No, he's not," Jessica retorted. "The coward took off when he saw me coming."

"He was scared," Andrew explained. "He was just playing. Is my mom going to be okay?"

"I think so. We haven't lost a mom to a doghouse yet."

Jessica sighed, her body tensing at the sudden sound of a power saw.

"You're not going to cut her in half, are you?" Andrew asked. "I saw them do it once on TV."

"Um. Now, that's an idea. What do you think, Bill?"

"A little messy, but you're the boss, Reed. Whatever you think."

"No. The chief probably wouldn't like it."

"Would you just get me out of here," Jessica snapped, her discomfort rising when his hand pushed against her bare side. The rough calluses of his palm felt cool against her hot skin. "What are you doing now?"

"Relax, I'm just trying to see if we have any room here. I think we'll cut the wood from the top down, maybe in a semicircle, and see if we can't rip the piece off around you. Just try to be still, okay?"

"I'm not going anywhere."

He laughed again. "No, I guess you're not. You know, I've always wanted a captive audience. Maybe I should try out my comedy routine on you. Did you hear the one about the fireman and the—?"

"Come on, McAllister. I want my breakfast," Bill interrupted.

"Relax, buddy. You could do with a few missed meals."

Jessica sighed as their banter continued. Would there be no end to her ordeal? "Would somebody please get me out of here," she yelled.

"Do you want to do the honors?" Reed asked.

"You go ahead," Bill replied. "I'm a little burned out from cutting women out of doghouses. Third one this week, isn't it?"

"Yeah, that's about right. Ma'am, I have to use a saw. Just keep your head down. We'll have you out in no time."

Jessica squeezed her eyes shut and offered a silent prayer as the saw cut into the wood well above her body but close enough to send a few doubts through her mind. As the pieces of wood were pulled off, she drew in clean, fresh breaths of air, suddenly realizing how little oxygen there had been in the doghouse. Finally, she felt a hand on her back, pulling at the wood until it gave, and she slithered out with relief.

Sitting back on her heels, she stared into a pair of smiling blue eyes that sparkled against tanned skin and sun-bleached hair. The man they belonged to was well built with strong, muscular arms and a broad chest, definitely all male, nothing like the kind of man she was familiar with. Self-consciously, her hand crept up to her red hair, calming the flyaway curls into some semblance of order.

He smiled approvingly. "Good, you're still in one piece. I'm Reed. That's Bill and Joe."

Jessica followed the tilt of his head, nodding awkwardly to the two men standing in her driveway. "Hello."

"Are you okay?" Reed asked. "Are you hurt anywhere? Do you want me to check you out?"

He leaned over and put his hands on her shoulders, and she immediately tensed. There was mischief in his eyes along with something else, something that she hadn't seen in any man's eyes in a very long time. Desire. Oh, Lord, not now, not when she had moved all the way across country to be on her own.

His fingers ran down her arms to her elbows and then lightly clasped her wrists.

"Feels good to me."

She drew in a deep breath as an echoing response rushed to her lips. Shaking her head, she pulled her hands away from his and jumped to her feet. It was then that she noticed the stricken expression on Andrew's face. His mouth was shaking as he tried to stop himself from crying. Lifting a finger, he pointed an accusatory hand at Reed.

"You broke my doghouse."

Reed stared at the little boy somberly. "I did, didn't I?" He squatted down next to Andrew. "I'm sorry. It was the only way I could get your mother out."

Andrew wiped a tear out of his eye with the rough edge of his fist. "My dad made it for me, and now it's broke."

"Maybe he can fix it," Reed suggested.

"He's not here. He's in Boston."

"It's okay," Jessica interrupted. "Wiley doesn't like to sleep in it anyway. He prefers my bed."

"Smart dog," Reed commented.

She sent him an irritated look and put her arm around Andrew's shoulders. "It's all right, honey. We'll get you a new doghouse."

"I don't want a new one. I want the one Daddy gave me. It's big and it's special."

"Maybe we can fix it," Jessica offered.

"You don't know how to fix it," he gulped. "And Daddy's not here."

Jessica sighed, reading the accusation clearly in his eyes. "Why don't we talk about this later, Andrew."

Andrew crossed his arms defiantly in front of his chest. "Fine."

Jessica shook her head and then looked at the three men who were taking in the scene with interest. She smoothed down the line of her skirt, trying to regain her sense of dignity. "Thank you for helping me. I really appreciate it. I don't know how else I would have gotten out of there."

"No problem. In fact, we specialize in cutting women out of doghouses."

Her lips tightened at Reed's light comment. "I hope I didn't take you away from something more important—like a fire. Please, don't let me keep you. I'm fine now." She hugged Andrew as he started to cry. "It will be all right. We'll get it fixed, don't worry."

Reed frowned as he looked at them. "Is there something I can do?"

"No. He'll be okay."

Reed didn't look like he believed her, but after a moment he shrugged and turned to his partners. "Ready guys?"

"Yeah. We're drawing quite a crowd out front," Bill commented. "Do you want to let your neighbors know you're okay?"

Jessica immediately shook her head, hating the idea of having anyone know what had happened to her. "I can't go out there like this."

Reed nodded with understanding. "We'll pass on the good word, don't worry."

"Thank you."

"No problem. Just part of the service."

The other two men had already disappeared out front, and Reed paused at the end of the yard, sending them both a long, searching look, then he turned and left. Jessica let out a sigh, feeling completely drained. Her legs weakened, and she stumbled over to a garden chair and sat down, pulling Andrew onto her lap. "I'm sorry, sweetie."

"I don't like it here," Andrew said again. "I want to go home."

"This is our home now."

"No, it's not. I want Daddy."

Jessica hugged him tightly. "I know you do. But this is going to work out best for all of us. You'll see."

For a moment she thought she had convinced him. His shoulders stopped trembling, and his body seemed to relax in her arms. Then he lifted his head and stared at her with watery eyes.

"Maybe Daddy will come out here to fix the doghouse for me," he said hopefully. "He could fly out on the airplane and then it wouldn't take so long to get here."

Jessica felt a stab of pain at the plea in his voice. Theodore wouldn't be coming out to San Diego, and he certainly wouldn't be interested in fixing a doghouse he had only bought to annoy her.

"He's working, Andrew. He can't take time off right now. You know how busy he is when school is in session."

"Maybe he could take a vacation. This is a good place to come. We could go to the beach together and build sand castles."

His innocent words filled her with emotion. If only they could. But there would be no more building of sand castles, not with Theodore. He had taken all of her dreams and smashed them like a tidal wave hitting the beach. And every time she had tried to build them back up, he had hit her again with more lies, more deceit. She could never trust him again, not where she was concerned and especially not where Andrew was concerned.

But how could she explain to her son what kind of man his father was without destroying his last bit of innocence? She just couldn't do it.

She set Andrew gently down on the ground, knowing the futility of their conversation. Only time and love would heal the hurt of their divorce. She couldn't do it all in a day. "Come on, sweetie. Let me get cleaned up and then I'll call the school and tell them we'll be late."

"I don't want to go to school."

"You love school, and it's the best place for us right now. We can forget this morning ever happened." She paused, looking around the yard. "Now, where is that dog? I want to make sure he stays out of trouble while we're gone."

"He's probably hiding under your bed," Andrew said, a reluctant smile hovering on his lips. "He likes your fuzzy slippers."

Her eyes rounded at the thought. "He better not touch my slippers. Not if he knows what's good for him."

"He's just playing, Mom. He's a puppy. I'm glad Daddy got him for me. He's my buddy."

Jessica shook her head, knowing she was beaten. Her slippers were probably in a dozen pieces by now, but at least Andrew had a friend. It was the first step in getting her son on the right track. She would figure out the rest later.

Chapter Two

Morning recess was just ending when they walked up the steps to Crestmoor Elementary. Jessica escorted Andrew to his class, taking a quick minute to explain his tardiness. She deliberately left out the details, and Andrew was still too preoccupied with the doghouse disaster to mention anything about the fire department being called to the house. Maybe, if she was lucky, no one would have to know.

She smiled to herself as she walked to her classroom. Who was she kidding? She had never been lucky. In fact, disaster seemed to follow her around. But she had a new life now. She was starting over. Things would change.

With a deliberately calm smile she opened the door to her classroom and sucked in a long deep breath as the noise level hit her like a clash of cymbals on a still night.

"Oh, thank goodness, you're here," Donna Anders wailed, as she tried to part two squabbling children engaged in a wrestling match on the floor.

"What on earth is going on?" Jessica asked.

"I wish I knew. Are they always like this?"

Jessica didn't have time to answer as a tiny figure flung her arms around Jessica's legs, sobbing hysterically. "Juanita, what's wrong?" She squatted down next to the child, drawing her into a warm, comforting hug.

The dark-haired little girl just stared back at her and continued to cry. In bewilderment, Jessica looked up at Donna who only shrugged helplessly.

"She's been that way all morning, ever since her sister, Rosa, left," Donna explained. "She just kept saying your name over and over. I tried to tell her you'd be coming in, but I don't think she understood me." Donna paused, her mouth falling open in astonishment as a little boy on the other side of the room picked up his truck and threw it at the wall. "Mitchell, don't do that." She started to move toward him when a ball hit her square between the shoulder blades. Throwing up her hands, she ran to the doorway. "They're all yours, Jessica. I quit. I'm going to stick to the front office from now on."

"Thanks for covering for me," Jessica replied, gathering Juanita into her arms, as she directed a quelling gaze across the room. "Mitchell, Conrad, Ryan and Blake. I want you on the carpet right now. Time out." Four little boys stopped in midstride and gave her uncertain looks, then one by one they sank to the floor.

Donna looked at her in amazement. "Wow! That was impressive."

Jessica smiled. "I taught kindergarten for two years before I came here. You have to learn fast if you want to survive. Now, if only I could do something for this little tyke." She ran a hand through Juanita's long, black hair. "It would be a lot easier if she spoke English. I did sign up for Spanish at the community college. I don't think I'm going to survive in this town if I can't communicate. Tonight is my first night."

"On Friday night? You're going to be in school?"

"Why not?"

Donna rolled her eyes. "Some women would find better things to do with their Friday nights, especially if they're single."

"I'm not single. I'm divorced. There is a difference. And the only thing I'm interested in right now is doing a good job here and getting my son to be a normal, happy little boy. Which means I better get back to work." Jessica began rapping out a series of orders. "Kimberly and Chelsea. I want those blocks cleaned up and put back in the box. Michael and Emily, turn the chairs right side up and push them back against the table. Marissa and Peter, you're responsible for putting the books back onto the shelf. And the rest of you put away whatever it is in your hands and take your place on the carpet."

The children began to move in one accord and Jessica nodded approvingly. "That's good. As soon as we get this room back to order, we'll have a story."

She turned to Donna who was still hovering in the doorway. "Thanks again."

"No problem. What happened to you, anyway?"

"It's a long story."

"So have lunch with me. You can tell me more about this class you're taking. Just think, you might meet an interesting man there."

"Would you stop? Enough with the men." Jessica's smile belied the harshness of her tone. Then it faded entirely as Timothy dumped his box of crayons on Megan's head. The little girl instantly screamed, setting off a chain reaction among some of the other children, including the one in her arms. "This is not my day, Donna. This is definitely not my day." She turned to the children. "Okay everybody. Let's have story time."

"Tell them the one about Prince Charming," Donna muttered as she slipped out the door. "It was always my favorite."

"I think I'll stick to Little Red Riding Hood and the Big Bad Wolf. I wouldn't want anyone taken in by a charming smile."

With that, Jessica walked over to the carpet and urged the children to sit in a circle in front of her. The cries eventually drifted away, and she dropped her voice down a notch as she debated what she wanted to say. "Once upon a time, there was a charming prince..." She cast a look over her shoulder to make sure Donna had left and then she continued with the story, watching their small faces light up with eagerness.

The classroom Jessica walked into later that night was a far cry from the colors and sounds of kindergarten. A dozen or so adults ranging in age from twenty to sixty filled the adult-size desks. They were sitting quietly, a few chatting about the unusually warm evening weather, the rest browsing through their textbooks or just looking aimlessly around.

"Buenas noches," the instructor said as she walked into the room. She was a dark-haired woman with black eyes and a bright vivacious smile. "Let's begin by repeating after me."

"Buenas días, buenas tardes, buenas noches," Jessica said gamely. "Good day, good afternoon, good evening." So far so good. She could handle this. In fact, school seemed to be the only place she felt comfortable these days. It was an environment she knew how to deal with. Her father had been a professor, her husband the same, and her mother had taught high school. Studying and learning was as common to her as eating and sleeping. There would be no surprises here, nothing she couldn't handle.

"Now, we're going to go around the room and say our names so that we can get better acquainted. I'll begin. *Me llamo* Theresa. My name is Theresa." The instructor smiled encouragingly at the man in the front row. "Next."

"Me . . . I forget the next part."

"Me llamo."

"Oh, right. *Me llamo* Harold."

Jessica smiled at his pronunciation, and turned inquiringly to the door when a sudden burst of air signaled the entrance of a late arrival. Her smile froze at the sight of the man framed in the doorway. He was wearing blue jeans and a San Diego State University T-shirt, but there was no mistaking the broad chest, the strong arms, or the wicked blue eyes.

She hastily looked away, as the teacher offered him a beaming smile.

"Buenas noches, señor."

"Sorry I'm late."

"Please, take a seat. We're just getting started."

Not here, not next to me, Jessica pleaded silently, her annoyance growing as he bypassed several chairs in the front of the room to slide into the desk next to hers.

"Hello there," he said with a smile.

Jessica nodded briefly, turning her attention back to the teacher.

"Let's continue," the instructor said. One by one the class members repeated their names.

When it got to be her turn, Jessica stumbled over the simple phrase, knowing that Reed was studying her quite openly. Finally, she got it out. "*Me llamo* Jessica."

"Jessica," he said softly as the teacher turned to the head of the next row. "I like it."

Jessica frowned and stared fixedly at the front of the room, waiting until it was his turn.

"*Me llamo* Reed," he said.

The instructor nodded as Reed finished the introductions in the class. "*¿Cómo está usted?*" she asked Reed.

"Huh?"

"I asked, how are you?"

"Oh, fine. Great." He flung a quick look in Jessica's direction. "In fact, I couldn't be better."

The instructor laughed. "Then open your books to page five, and we'll begin with some basic phrases. I want you all to realize how wonderful it is to be able to communicate in another language. I think you'll be pleasantly surprised at how much fun this class will be."

"I already am," whispered Reed.

Jessica's breath caught at the murmured words, and her heart fluttered against her chest. He was flirting with her, and he was very good at it. Her battered ego couldn't help but respond to the sexy invitation in his eyes. It had been a long time since anyone had given her such a look. But what to do about it was another question. Shaking her head, she stared down at her book and concentrated on repeating the instructor's commands.

"Hey, wait up," Reed shouted after her as she walked quickly down the hall. Her escape would have been complete if a door hadn't opened in front of her, allowing another class to pour out into the hall. By the time she reached the top of the stairs Reed was right next to her, his athletic stride having no trouble keeping pace with hers.

"How are you feeling?" he asked.

"Fine." She offered him a brief smile and continued briskly down the stairs, hoping that he would somehow be cut off before they reached the outside door. Unfortunately, he was right on her heels as they walked out into the sultry night air.

"What's your hurry, Jessica?"

"I need to get home." She flung the words over her shoulder, hoping he would take the hint. He didn't. Instead he jogged along next to her, his legs moving fluidly in his faded blue jeans.

"How's your son? Is he still upset about the doghouse?"

"He'll be all right."

"I'm sorry we had to cut through it. I really didn't see any other way to get you out."

She flushed at the memory and kept walking, refusing to look him in the eye. "I just want to forget it. I can't believe you showed up in this class."

"Don't worry, your secret is safe with me. I never tell tales out of the firehouse."

"That's comforting."

"So what's the problem? Why don't you want to talk to me?" Reed put a hand on her shoulder forcing her to stop walking.

Her head swiveled around in anger as she prepared to tell him to keep his hands to himself, but when she looked into his eyes, the breath seemed to drain from her body. He adjusted his hand on her shoulder, and an irrepressible tingle ran down her spine.

She hated the way she was responding to him as if she had no control over her emotions. If there was anything she had learned in the past couple of years, it was never to allow anyone to have control over her again.

Deliberately, she took a step back, forcing his arm to fall back to his side, as she tried to answer him politely but firmly. "It's not that I don't want to talk to you, I just..." Her words faded away. How could she tell this man that she didn't trust his blue eyes or his winning smile, that she had never flirted with any man except her husband and look where that had gotten her? It was hardly the stuff polite lies were made of, but for the life of her she just couldn't think of anything to say.

"You don't have to be embarrassed about this morning," Reed said, breaking into the lengthening silence. "I've seen worse, believe me."

She shifted her feet uncomfortably, trying to find something to look at besides him. "I'm sure you have.

It's just that I felt like a fool, and all you did was make jokes."

"I know. I wanted you to relax."

Her gaze flew up to meet his. "Relax? You've got to be kidding."

"I'm not. I never know how someone is going to react in a crisis. Some women might have freaked out being stuck in such a tight space. I didn't know what was going through your head, so I thought it best to try to take your mind off the situation."

Jessica stared at him warily, not sure whether she could trust his explanation. "Really? I'm sure it must have looked pretty funny to you with my... body hanging out that way."

Reed smiled, his eyes twinkling at her with open enjoyment. "I have to admit, you do have great legs."

Jessica's mouth dropped open, and she quickly shut it. Then she said, "That's not very professional."

"I'm off duty."

"Look, I have to go."

"Why? Do you have someone waiting for you?"

"My son," she replied sharply, ignoring the speculative gleam in his eyes.

"Is he the only one?"

"Yes, not that it's any of your business."

"Okay. I'll change the subject. Why are you taking Spanish? Are you planning a trip to Acapulco, maybe some dancing to a mariachi band?"

She smiled as his words created a lovely but impossible picture in her mind. To be that carefree—what a whimsical thought. "No. I'm a kindergarten teacher, and there's a little girl in my class that I want to be able to talk to. We've gotten close, and I know she trusts me, but I can't help her until I find out what's really wrong."

"Being able to speak Spanish may not help you. Five-year-olds seem to have a language of their own."

"I kind of like their language. At least it's honest."

Reed sent her a curious look. "You're not from here, are you? I hear a trace of an accent in your voice, but I can't quite pinpoint it."

"I'm from Boston."

He studied her thoughtfully. "Oh. That explains it."

"Explains what?"

His lazy smile returned as he pointed to her collar. "The buttoned-up look, the proper tone in your voice. You're a long way from home."

"Yes, I am. It's the way I want it. And I happen to like this shirt, buttons and all."

"And how do you like my hometown?"

She hesitated at the question, knowing it was crazy to keep talking to him. It was obvious that they were as different as Solana Beach and Boston. But her feet wouldn't seem to move. He was too close. His shoulders were too broad; his eyes were too blue. He made her feel . . .

"Hot. It's very hot here." She waved a hand in front of her face to fan the still night air.

He smiled at her answer, taking another step closer, until his chest was just a breath away from her pounding heart. He wasn't touching her, but in another second . . .

"It is hot," Reed said, his husky voice implying much more than the weather. "In fact, the heat down here has a tendency to bring out all kinds of strange emotions. You might even find yourself unbuttoning that top button.''

Her fingers crept up to her neckline subconsciously. If only she could look away. What was so compelling about his eyes? She had blue eyes. She looked into the mirror every morning when she did her makeup. There was nothing particularly magical about the color, no magnetic attraction, so why couldn't she look away? Why couldn't she tell him to go and leave her alone?

"It's too hot to fight," Reed murmured. "I'd give in if I were you."

"You're not me, and I'll deal with the heat in my own way." She paused, hating the way her voice had gotten emotional and high. What had happened to her calm and cool? She took in a deep breath and let it out. "Why are you taking this class?"

"I'm thinking about doing some bullfighting."

She stared at him in amazement. "You're kidding, right?"

He shrugged. "Maybe not. We're not too far from the Mexican border, and I'm always up for a challenge."

"You're crazy."

"I thought women loved bullfighters. There's something dangerous and exciting about a man ready to face a mad bull, don't you think?"

"No." She shook her head emphatically. "I think it's the stupidest thing I've ever heard of."

"Then I guess I'll have to fall back on my other reason for taking Spanish. I want to be able to communicate on the job. There are a lot of people in this town who don't speak English, and when we get into a crisis situation with a person who can't understand us, it can get very scary."

His voice turned serious as did his expression, which only baffled her more. "I'm sure it does. Good night, Mr. McAllister." She turned and walked quickly to her car, fighting back the urge to run.

"*Buenas noches,* Jessica," Reed called after her. "*Está muy bonita.*" The husky Spanish words sang through the night like a lullaby, and for a moment, Jessica stared blankly at the keyhole in the car door. When she finally turned around he was gone, and she was sorry.

For the first time in a long time she felt alive again, dangerously alive. It reminded her of the way she had felt when she and Theo had first met, those incredibly exciting days of courtship when she had truly believed the handsome professor loved her. But she had been a child then, barely twenty. Now, she was a grown woman with a child of her own. She couldn't afford to make the same mistake twice. She couldn't risk falling in love again. She would have to keep her distance and brush him off. Reed McAllister was a gorgeous hunk of man. He wouldn't waste time on a dead end. She would just say no. It was really that simple.

"Never!" Reed shouted, the wind blowing the words back in his face in mockery. The white froth of the ocean wave whipped around his bare legs in a cold, stinging fashion, but balancing on his surfboard, Reed felt only an incredible sense of exhilaration as he battled the elements. He bent his knees and urged the board farther along the crest of the wave. For a split second he thought he was the victor, the conquering hero, but then his board hit a rough edge of water and he lost control, spinning over the back of the wave and plunging beneath the water.

The ocean pounded him down, punishing him for having thought even for an instant that he could win. It wasn't until his knees scraped along the sandy bottom that he managed to force his head above water and take a long, welcome breath. His heart was still pounding as he reached for his surfboard and walked out of the water to where his friend was waiting.

"At least the board didn't hit you on the head, although it might have knocked some sense into you." Bill Carlton pushed his sunglasses to the top of his balding head as Reed set his board down on the sand.

"It was a hell of a ride. I'll say that. If this kind of weather holds into October, there will be plenty of good days out here. Maybe I can even get you in the water. You're beginning to look like a beached whale."

"Thanks. You're a real pal. You know that kid took it all the way in." Bill motioned his head toward a thin seventeen-year-old grandstanding on his surfboard.

Reed frowned. "No way. He's a punk. He couldn't handle a wave like that."

"That's what they used to say about us—about fifteen years ago." Bill tossed him a towel. "But you still have some nice moves. At least that's what my cousin Tracy said."

Reed snapped the towel against Bill's bare stomach. "Watch your mouth, buddy."

"It was a compliment."

"Yeah, right." Reed sat down heavily on his towel and for a moment they were both content to stare out at the surf. "I think I'll go back out," he said finally.

Bill sent him a sharp look. "What are you trying to do—kill yourself? You've been out there for hours. I was thinking more along the lines of getting some breakfast."

"You go ahead. I'm not very hungry this morning."

"And leave you here alone?"

Reed made a sarcastic face. "If I need help, I'll yell for the kid out there. I've got some thinking to do."

"About what, or should I say who?"

Reed considered the question thoughtfully, picking up a handful of sand and letting it drift through fingers. "I got a call from Larry. There's an opening in New York City. It would mean a promotion, more money, excitement, adventure, the chance to—"

"The chance to get yourself killed. They've got some tough buildings there. Plus, you'd have to live in New York City. They don't have any waves there."

Reed sent him a quick smile. "That's my main concern."

"Yeah, right."

"But I've spent my whole life in this town. I can walk down the street and see somebody I know at every corner."

"What's wrong with that?"

"I don't know. Maybe I need a change. I feel . . ." He shrugged his shoulders, searching for the right words. "Restless. Like something is missing, something important."

"And you think it's in New York? I thought Elizabeth went to San Francisco."

Reed shot him an irritated look. "This doesn't have anything to do with her leaving. That was a mutual decision. She wanted marriage, and I didn't."

"Why not?"

"I'm too young to die."

"It's not that bad. I know you had it tough growing up, but—"

Reed stood up abruptly. "That doesn't have anything to do with it. I'm going to take a ride. I'll see you around."

"Watch yourself, McAllister. You don't have nine lives."

"Says who?"

Bill shook his head in despair. "We're going to be thirty-five next year, middle age. It's time to start thinking about security and pension plans, maybe even children. We're not kids anymore."

Reed laughed. "You think about it. I'll worry about tomorrow when and if it comes."

"Just wait. Your time will come. The right woman, and snap." He snapped his fingers for emphasis. "It's all over."

Reed ignored his comment and picked up his board. "Right now all I want to think about is landing the next big wave. Go on, get out of here, and don't worry, I won't do anything stupid."

Chapter Three

He *was* doing something stupid. Running into a fire without taking the proper precautions, he could get burned badly. The thought made him pause, and Reed leaned against the door of his Jeep Wrangler as he studied the simple ranch-style house in front of him.

Jessica Blake wasn't exactly a fire, but there was something about that redhead that made his blood boil. Her hair was a challenging flame, but her voice was pure ice. What a challenge—what a gorgeous challenge. Of course, she'd probably give him another polite brush-off, maybe even shut the door in his face—not slam, but close firmly.

If he had any sense, he would walk away. She was alone with a kid, a woman with encumbrances. She probably had long-term plans, life insurance, maybe even a will. What the hell was he thinking of?

He smiled to himself, remembering the moment when he pulled her from the doghouse. Her blue eyes had been flashing with embarrassment and anger, her red hair a perfect frame for her oval face, her long, shapely legs disappearing beneath her skirt. The early morning rescue was indelibly printed on his mind.

She would hate knowing that. Jessica wasn't the kind of woman who enjoyed losing her dignity. In fact, she seemed to wear it like a fireproof suit, which only made her more intriguing. Maybe if he hadn't seen her in complete disarray, heard passion and anger in her voice, maybe then the ice would have frozen him out. But he had caught a glimpse, and he wanted to see more. It was a risk, but what the hell, he lived on risks. They could have a good time together. He could loosen her up, unbutton those buttons....

He began to walk slowly toward the house, noting the newly planted garden along the walkway, the carefully swept front porch and the garden basket filled with wildflowers hanging from the awning. Neat and tidy with a hint of color, a touch of daring, but not enough to draw attention, to be really bold. He wondered what it would take to get her to cross the line of politeness, to let her hair down. He had a feeling the result would be pretty incredible.

Pushing his index finger down hard on the bell, he let it ring, once, twice and then three times. Maybe he was worried about nothing. Maybe she'd be happy to see him.

Jessica was in the middle of changing the bag in the vacuum cleaner when the shrill bell pealed through the house. The sudden noise caught her off guard, and her hands pulled sharply at the bag sending a cloud of dust and dirt billowing into her face.

"Darn," she muttered, coughing as the dust got into her lungs. The doorbell rang again and again. With a resigned look at the dirt now layered across her coral colored T-shirt and faded blue jeans, she strode over to the door and pulled it open.

Reed's face split into a wide grin as they faced each other. "Hello again."

"What are you doing here?" Jessica asked in astonishment, her hands flying up to her dirty face, as his glance travelled down her body. "I was in the middle of cleaning."

"What were you cleaning—the chimney?"

"No, I was vacuuming. Actually, I was changing the bag, and the doorbell caught me off guard. It's your fault."

"It usually is. Can I come in anyway?"

"Why?"

"I'd like to talk to you, and maybe offer some help."

"I don't need any help, and I really don't have time to talk. I'm in the middle of cleaning, and then I have to get lunch for Andrew." Her words came to an abrupt halt. "The eggs," she said wildly, making a dash for the kitchen.

Reed looked at her in bemusement and then followed her inside. By the time he got to the kitchen she was staring in disgust at a blackened pot while one hand waved through a cloud of smoke hovering over the stove.

He peered over her shoulder at a mess of egg whites and yolks. "I hope that's not lunch."

"It was going to be," she said dismally, slamming the pot down on the stove. "This is not my day. In fact, this is not my week, my month or even my year." Her voice rose with agitation and then halted as his gaze caught hers. "I'm sorry. I guess I got carried away."

"Sounds like you're entitled. Have things really been that bad?"

"Yes." She paused, reaching out to open the window. The fresh breeze lightened the tension in the room and gave her a chance to regain her poise. "What are you doing here?"

He held up the toolbox in his hands. "I thought maybe I could fix the doghouse for you."

She sent him a long, searching look. "You don't have to do that."

"I know I don't have to. But I couldn't stop thinking about the look on your son's face. Kids respect fire fighters, and I'd hate to think I destroyed that."

"It wasn't your fault. You had to get me out."

"True, but maybe I can make things right. I've got a piece of wood in the Jeep that I think will fit perfectly on the front of the doghouse with a few minor adjustments."

While he was talking, he reached out almost absentmindedly and stroked a smear of dust off the side of her cheek. His touch took her by surprise, and she had to resist the urge to turn her face into the warm caress of his palm. Whatever he was saying went completely by her. All of her senses were focused on the simple caress of his hand against her cheek, such a gentle gesture, and yet such a provocative one.

"Jessica?"

Her gaze flew to his face in a startled fashion. "What?"

He smiled at her so warmly that she could feel a wave of heat generating between them. It was tempting to move closer, to lose herself in the warmth. She had been out in the cold for so long.

"I asked if you wanted me to get started now."

Get started? The question screamed at her as a dozen meanings fled through her mind. She took in a deep breath and silently scolded herself for getting carried away. "You're not working today?"

"No. I'm off until tomorrow. Our schedule varies each week. I'm hoping I'll be able to make the most of my Spanish classes, but maybe I can copy your notes if I have to miss one."

"Sure," she said casually, trying to bring her pulse back under control. "That's no problem."

"Maybe we can study together sometime, too."

Her lips curved into an unwilling smile. "This is beginning to sound like a conversation I heard going on outside my classroom between two sixth graders."

Reed chuckled. "I'll bet you hear a lot of interesting conversations."

"Sometimes. The kids are so grown up now. It's scary, especially when I look at Andrew and think how quickly time is passing." She shook her head, trying to keep her emotions at bay. "It will be difficult to let him go."

"He's only seven."

"I know, but it seems like yesterday that he was a baby. You'll understand someday when you have a child."

His expression turned grim. "I don't think so. I'm not planning on having any kids."

"Why not?" Her question came out before she could stop it. The thought of anyone not wanting a child was totally beyond her.

"It's a long story. Where is Andrew, anyway?"

"He's doing some schoolwork in his room."

Reed raised one eyebrow. "On a gorgeous Saturday like this? He should be outside, getting some fresh air. Are you one of those slave-driver moms?"

"No, I'm not. Actually, I encouraged him to go outside, but he's working on his computer, and he really enjoys it." Jessica knew her tone was filled with defensiveness, but Reed's comments were so close to her own guilty feelings that she couldn't help but react.

"Whatever you say." Reed moved toward the back door. "I'll get started on the doghouse, unless you want some help with the cleanup?" He motioned toward the pan on the stove, and she shook her head.

"No. I'll just toss it in the garbage and start over." Her words brought a wry smile to her lips. "The story of my life."

"I think I'd like to hear it sometime."

"No, you wouldn't." She paused. "Whatever you can do for the doghouse would be greatly appreciated. It means a lot to Andrew."

"Because his father gave it to him?"

"Yes."

"And is his father going to be joining you out here?"

She shook her head and walked over to the stove, busying her hands with the cleanup. "No, we're divorced."

"How long?"

"A little over a year." She swung around to face him. "Why all the personal questions?"

"It's the only way I know to get answers." He paused at the back door. "Does my fixing the doghouse earn me a lunch invitation?"

"You've already seen one effort. Are you sure you want to risk it?"

He nodded slowly, his eyes capturing hers in a long, enticing look. "I'm a risk taker, Jess. I like to live on the edge, something you should probably know about me right now."

His words went far deeper than a simple response to lunch, and the tension between them returned. "I don't even like to look over the edge. Maybe you should know that about me, too."

"You? A woman who moves all the way across country on her own? Crawls into a doghouse after her wallet? Takes Spanish classes at night?" He shook his head. "Sounds to me like a woman who's at least thinking about taking a look."

She turned her back on him, ignoring the speculation in his eyes. "You don't know the first thing about me."

"Maybe not, but I'd like to."

Jessica was trying to think of an easy reply when he slipped out the door, shutting it quietly behind him.

Twenty minutes later, Jessica had made tuna fish sandwiches and cut up a bowl of fruit. With the lunch made, she had nothing to distract her from the sound of hammering going on in the backyard. Giving in to a needling urge, she shifted the curtain to one side and looked out the window.

Reed was holding the piece of wood up against the doghouse, measuring the width with his eyes. She could see the muscles in his back working against the thin material of his T-shirt as he adjusted the wood to fit into the allotted space. He was perspiring from the heat, and his cheeks were red, revealing the stubble of beard along his jawline. All in all, he was a very physical man and she was struck once again by the striking contrast to her ex-husband.

Theodore had been attractive in his own way—pale-skinned with serious gray eyes and always closely shaven. His hands had been smooth and fine, his nails clipped appropriately. When he had come to bed he had always taken a shower first and combed his hair. Theo had been refined, sophisticated. Reed was...

She dropped her hand and let the curtain slide back into place. Closing her eyes, she leaned back against the counter and tried to stop the rush of emotions that had suddenly sprung forth. Reed was just the opposite of Theo. That's why he was attractive to her. He was not her type. Just because she had imagined what it would be like to get close to all that heat did not mean she was going to do anything about it. She couldn't risk getting burned, not again.

With that thought in mind, she walked out into the hall and called for Andrew.

"Yes, Mom?" He came out onto the landing and she smiled up at him.

"Lunch is ready, honey."

"I'm not hungry."

Jessica's smile faded at the depression lurking in his voice. "I made tuna fish sandwiches, your favorite."

"Do I have to?"

"Yes. And I have another surprise for you, too."

"What?"

"Why don't you come down and find out?" Jessica suggested.

Andrew whistled for Wiley and the two came the stairs, one with enthusiasm and one with o reluctance. When Andrew got closer to the kitchen, his expression grew curious.

"What's that noise?"

"Hammering," she said with a smile. She followed Andrew over to the back door, eager to see his expression. She hoped Reed's efforts would bring some of the life back to her son.

Andrew opened the back door and stared at the scene, a wide grin slowly spreading across his face. "Oh, wow! My doghouse!"

Andrew ran into the backyard as Reed hammered in the final nail. Although the front piece of wood was a slightly different color, the house was well put together and almost as good as new.

Reed smiled at Andrew. "What do you think?"

Before Andrew could say a word, Wiley barked approvingly and they all laughed.

"I guess his opinion is the one that matters most," Reed replied, pulling the wiggly dog into his arms. "This is your home, pal, but we don't want any more stolen goods inside. Got that?"

Wiley barked again and scampered out of reach, into the dark confines of the doghouse.

"What do you say, Andrew?" Jessica prompted.

Andrew looked at Reed with a serious expression on his face. "Thank you for fixing it."

"You're welcome."

Andrew got down on his knees and peered inside. "It looks pretty good."

"Don't go in there," Jessica warned. "One person stuck in the doghouse is enough."

Reed smiled up at her. "I fixed that, too." He pointed to the hinges on the side and at the top. "The small door is for Wiley, but if for some reason you need to get in there, you can take the roof off. It's on hinges now. I must say, this is a huge house for such a small dog."

"I know, but we got the house first and the dog second. Not very good planning, I guess. Too bad it wasn't big enough for me, but I won't be going in there again. I learned my lesson."

"Yes, but did Wiley learn his?"

"I doubt it." Jessica turned her head away from his inviting smile. "Andrew, why don't you go wash your hands? I've got lunch ready."

"Are you going to eat with us?" he asked Reed.

"He already invited himself," Jessica replied with a dry look in Reed's direction as Andrew ran into the house.

He grinned. "I'd have starved if I'd waited for you."

"It's nothing fancy."

"Doesn't matter to me. I'm a fireman. I can eat anything…except my own cooking." He followed her into the house and washed his hands at the kitchen sink as she laid the plates on the table.

Sitting down at the large oak table, he looked around the warm, cozy room and smiled. "This is nice, Jess. Feels like a home."

"That's what I want it to be," she said, joining him at the table. "I never had a chance before to decorate the way I wanted to. My husband preferred a professional touch to mine."

Reed raised an eyebrow. "Really? I bet you have a very nice touch."

She cleared her throat. "I just know what I like, warm colors and comfortable furniture. Anyway, it was hard to move Andrew away from Boston, so I'm trying to make it a nice transition. I want him to be happy here. Sometimes I wish . . .'' She stopped as she saw him watching her with interest. ''Never mind.''

''What were you going to say?''

''Nothing, forget it.''

''Jess . . .''

''My name is Jessica,'' she corrected.

''You look like a Jess.''

''What do you mean?''

''Nothing, forget it.''

''That's not fair.''

Andrew entered the kitchen with a curious look. ''What's not fair, Mom?''

Jessica shook her head and pushed Andrew's plate toward his end of the table. ''Did you finish your homework?''

''Yes.''

''Good, then I was thinking we could go to the mall later today, maybe get an ice cream.''

''I think I'll just work on my computer.''

''You can do that later, tonight, when it's dark,'' Jessica said, trying to ignore Reed's speculative looks. ''You've been in your room all day.''

''She's right, Andrew. Although I think I'd pass on the mall. Why not check out the beach, maybe throw a Frisbee around with Wiley?'' Reed suggested.

''I don't know how to throw one.''

''Your mom can teach you.''

Andrew looked at Reed and then wrinkled up his nose. ''I don't think so.''

Reed glanced over at Jessica. ''You don't know how to throw one, either?''

"It's not a crime," she retorted. "But I'm sure I could figure it out, if that's what Andrew would like to do. Is it, honey?"

Andrew shrugged as if he didn't care one way or the other. "It doesn't matter."

"Tell you what, how about if I take both of you down to the beach and give you some expert tips on Frisbee throwing? I'll even provide the disc," Reed offered.

"We don't want to take up all your time," Jessica replied hastily and then felt guilty as she saw the momentary spark on Andrew's face fade away. He hadn't shown much interest in anything since they had moved to California, and she desperately wanted to get him out of the rut her husband and nanny had created in Boston.

"I'm free all day," Reed said. "And I think you two could use a run on the beach."

"Excuse me? Do I look like a dog?"

Reed laughed. "Hardly. I meant it figuratively speaking. Come on, you've got the big, beautiful ocean practically at your back door. Why go to the mall and shuffle around with the crowds?"

"It does sound tempting." She paused for a long moment, feeling somewhat uncomfortable under his direct gaze. "I just don't want you to get the wrong idea."

"And what would that be?"

"That I'm encouraging you."

"You're definitely not doing that. What are you so afraid of? Don't men and women go out together in Boston?"

"Yes, but they don't usually meet the way we did. I don't even know you."

"And I don't know you. That's what's so great about this idea."

His simple explanation made her smile. "What do you think, Andrew? It does sound fun. We've only been to the beach once since we moved here."

"Once? You've got to be kidding," Reed said in amazement. "In that case, you two are definitely in need of the Reed McAllister personal beach tour. I can guarantee you a good time, Andrew. Just give me the thumbs up, and we'll be on our way."

Andrew hesitated. "Can Wiley come, too?"

"Of course he can."

"All right. I'll go get my sweater." Andrew slid out of his chair and walked quietly out of the room.

"I hope this isn't an imposition," Jessica said.

"I don't do anything that I don't want to do."

She raised her eyebrows at his cocky tone. "Lucky you."

"Luck doesn't have anything to do with it." Reed pushed his chair back. "Besides, it will be nice to have your son along on our first date."

Jessica stared at him in disbelief. "This is not a date."

"It isn't?"

"No. It's an outing with—friends."

"At least we're friends, I guess that's something. Last night you were barely speaking to me."

"Probably because I barely know you," Jessica replied. "Tell me, do you flirt with every woman you rescue?"

Reed grinned. "Only the pretty ones." He walked over to the kitchen door and called up to Andrew. "Get a move on, buddy. We're losing daylight." He turned back to Jessica. "You know, he doesn't need a sweater. It's hot out there."

"It's a habit with him. He isn't used to the weather here." Jessica looked down at her soiled clothes. "Maybe I'll throw on something cleaner. It will just take a minute. You don't mind, do you? I'll hurry."

"Take whatever time you need, Jess." He folded his arms across his chest and leaned back against the counter with a complacent smile. "I'm not going anywhere."

That's what she was afraid of, Jessica realized, as she jogged up the stairs to her room. But it wasn't like she had agreed to dinner at a romantic candlelit restaurant. They were going to throw a disc on the beach with Andrew and Wiley. What could possibly go wrong?

Chapter Four

The bright orange disc sailed through the air, lifting higher as the wind carried it farther down the beach. Jessica ran backward, laughing as strands of hair blew in front of her eyes. She was going to catch this one. She was absolutely determined.

It was coming down now. One more step, maybe two and she would have it. She reached up her hand and then stumbled backward as a large male body barreled into her.

She collapsed on the sand, the breath knocked out of her as Reed fell on top of her. The orange Frisbee landed just over their heads.

"Whoops," Reed said with a chuckle. "I guess I got a little too close to you."

Jessica's chest heaved as she tried to regain some air into her lungs. "Would you get off me before I suffocate?"

Reed pulled back only slightly, taking the majority of his weight off her but still keeping her captive on the ground. "I think I like you this way." His eyes roamed over her flushed face, the sparkle in her eyes, the messy hair. "You look fabulous." His gaze drifted down to her blue knit shirt with the tiny buttons that ran all the way down to her waist. "Even if you are still buttoned up." He raised his head and looked back at Andrew. "Can you get the Frisbee, buddy? Your mom needs to catch her breath."

"I could do that better if you got off me," Jessica muttered, swallowing hard when he looked back into her eyes.

"One kiss. Just one kiss."

"No way. Andrew—"

"Is throwing it to Wiley," he finished.

Jessica could have moved, if she'd wanted to. His arms weren't holding her down, only his gaze. But she felt so alive, as if she had awakened after a long, cold winter. The heat of the sun warmed her face, and she could feel the gritty texture of the sand burning into the back of her neck. There was salt in the air. She wondered if she would taste it on his lips. But he still hadn't kissed her. He just kept looking at her in a strange, unfathomable way. She wondered why.

"Mom, are you okay?"

Andrew's innocent question filled her with guilt and embarrassment. What on earth was she doing, rolling around in the sand with a perfect stranger when her son was looking on?

"She's fine, just got the wind knocked out of her," Reed answered easily, sliding off to one side. "That was a nice throw, Andrew. You're good at this."

Andrew's eyes lit up. "Do you think so? I didn't throw it too high or too wide?"

"It was perfect." Reed threw an arm around Andrew and dragged him down to the ground in a mock wrestling fashion. "In fact, you showed me up, kid, and you know what that means?"

Andrew looked up at him in bewilderment.

"I can either toss you in the ocean and let the sharks go after you or..." He paused dramatically. "I can tickle you to death." Reed pounced on him, tickling him under his arms and around the stomach.

Andrew giggled and tried to fight him off. Jessica watched the two of them in amazement. She had never seen Andrew roughhouse with anyone, and Reed was so good with him, so natural. She felt a tug at her heart, wishing Andrew's father could have shared such a simple moment with his son.

But he wouldn't have cared, wouldn't have seen the point in anything that wasn't connected to his interests and getting ahead. He would have been worried about dirt getting onto his pants or Andrew shirking his studies.

Thank God she had come to her senses and broken the ties. At least Andrew and she had a chance now to love each other without rules and endless propriety and a too-efficient nanny always stepping between them.

She knew it would take time. Andrew still hadn't forgiven her for the divorce or moving away from Boston, but maybe someday he would understand. She smiled at his squeal of pleasure. It was the first time in a long time she had seen such animation in his face.

"Now, I've got you," Andrew said triumphantly, pushing Reed onto his back, and sitting across his chest, his tiny hands pressing against the strong muscles in Reed's arms as he held him down.

"All right. I give up," Reed groaned, flicking a glance over at Jessica. "Aren't you going to help me?"

She shook her head, grinning back at him. "No way."

"That's gratitude for you. I rescue you from a woman-eating doghouse and you're just going to sit there and let your son tickle me to death?"

"I'll make him stop before he kills you."

"Great, thanks." Reed groaned as Andrew began an attack on his armpits. Then Wiley dived into the fray, barking with glee as his teeth clamped down on the edge of Reed's shirt. Jessica burst out laughing, ignoring the warning glint in his eyes that told her she was going to be in big trouble later on. Finally, Reed freed himself and jumped to his feet. "Last one to the pier has to buy dinner."

Reed swept Andrew off his feet and took off at a dead run as Jessica struggled to get up. By the time she reached the pier, Reed, Andrew and Wiley were resting on the bench.

"That wasn't fair," she protested. "You had a head start."

"Maybe, but it was fun," Reed said. "Where are we going for dinner? I'm in the mood for pizza."

"Pizza, yeah!" Andrew clapped his hands. "I want pepperoni." Wiley barked his approval and Jessica looked in wonderment at her usually introverted child.

"What do you say, Jess?"

She threw up her hands. "I give up. Pizza it is."

Andrew slid off the bench and ran ahead of them to the car with Wiley following close behind. When he was out of earshot, Jessica turned to Reed. "Thank you for today. I haven't seen Andrew so happy in a long time."

"He is a quiet kid."

"Too quiet. But that's going to change. I want him to do things like this, run on the beach and make friends and get dirty. He was on his own too much in Boston."

"Why was that?"

Reed's probing question made her realize how much she was revealing, and her guard immediately came up. "It was just the situation. Do you know a good pizza place around here?"

Reed accepted her change of subject with a wry smile. "Do I know a good pizza place? I happen to be an expert on pizza."

"And an expert on Frisbee disc throwing. You do have a lot of talents."

"Yeah, I'm hoping I can show them all to you."

Jessica's breath caught at his words. "I think I'll quit with the pizza."

"What are you scared of?" he asked, his smile fading into something more serious.

"Me? Scared?" She thought about the question, and this time it was she who smiled. "I used to be afraid of everything—saying the wrong words, doing the wrong thing, wearing the wrong dress, even driving the wrong kind of car. Let me tell you, it was exhausting."

"And now?"

"Now? Now, I'm just afraid of liking the wrong person." She met his gaze head on. "That would really hurt. I know, I've been there."

Reed stared back at her. "So have I. Now, why don't we get the pizza?"

Reed's cryptic words ran around in her mind during their loud, crazy meal at the pizza parlor. She wondered about his past, and if he had been involved with someone or even married. He certainly seemed to know a lot of people, and the waitresses all called him by name, giving him special attention. Reed just took it in stride, spending most of his time talking to Andrew.

When the pizza plate was empty and the pitcher of root beer down to the last drop, Andrew slid off the bench and politely asked Jessica for a quarter to play a video game. Jessica opened her mouth to say no, but before she could get an answer out, Reed had pulled out three quarters and handed them to Andrew, who quickly walked away.

"I wish you hadn't done that," Jessica said.

Reed looked at her in surprise. "Why not?"

"Because video games can become an obsession. I don't want Andrew to get caught up in them."

"He plays computer games. What's the difference?"

"Those are educational."

"I still don't see the harm in a couple of video games. They're challenging and fun."

"Is fun all you can think about?"

"When I'm at a pizza parlor, yes."

Jessica's lips clamped together in a tight line. "I would appreciate it if you would let me make the decisions about Andrew in the future."

"Fine. I didn't think it was that big of a deal. Frankly, I just wanted to spend some time alone with you."

She stiffened at his words, the noise of the restaurant surrounding them like a warm cocoon. He had leaned closer so she could hear him, and she had leaned closer in response. Now they were too close, too intimate. What was she doing? She sat back in her seat, directing her gaze to Andrew, hoping Reed would take a hint and leave it alone, but of course he didn't.

"I'd like to go out with you, just the two of us."

Jessica stared straight ahead. "I'm not interested in dating anyone. I thought I had made that clear."

"I'm not anyone, and we had a good time today. You have to admit that."

Jessica turned to face him. "If you thought you could get to me through Andrew—"

"No, I didn't think that," Reed said forcefully. "I don't use kids to get to their mothers. I happen to think your son needs some lightening up, and he looks a lot happier now, don't you think?"

Her temper flared. "I can take care of my own son. And if he has problems, I will deal with them."

Reed held up a hand. "Whoa, Jess. Slow down. I'm not trying to tell you how to raise your son. Believe me, that is the *last* thing I want to do." He paused, considering her troubled face. "What's going on? I get the feeling you're reacting to more than just me."

Jessica took a deep breath and slowly let it out, silently admitting the truth of his words. "I'm sorry if

I jumped down your throat. Maybe we should go home.''

"And maybe you should talk to me. I bet it has something to do with your ex."

"Theo was very controlling," Jessica admitted after a long pause. "He had definite ideas about what he wanted for Andrew, and I didn't have much of a say in anything. He hired a nanny for Andrew when he was two years old, and I was forced into a secondary role. I started feeling like the outsider, not the mother. I'd make a suggestion and everyone would ignore it. I guess it's a bit of a sore spot with me."

"I guess so."

"That's the reason why I moved to California," she continued. "I want Andrew to grow up in a place that is a little looser, not so many rules, so much pressure on achievement. Not that I don't think there is a place for rules and such, but our lives were so restricted before. I sometimes felt like a sneeze would bring the place down, and I'm sure Andrew must have felt the same way. Or if he didn't, he should have. That's why I had to go. It was the best decision." Jessica shook her head in frustration, realizing that she was still defending her actions. "Of course, Andrew hated me for taking him away from his father and his nanny and the few friends that he had at the academy."

"The academy?"

"The prep school he was attending."

"He's seven years old, and he was going to an academy? You are tough."

"Not me, Theo. I was totally against it, but he convinced me that Andrew would get a good solid education there. Then I found out they believed in spanking and physical punishment. The first time he came home in tears with his bottom paddled, I knew that I couldn't stand by and do nothing."

"Good for you."

"Not really. I should have done it sooner. But I didn't know how to fight Theo. I was raised in a very traditional household. My mother always gave in to my father's wishes. It was expected. I was twenty-one years old when I got married. It took me a while to figure out that Theo was the one who was wrong, not me. I was taking everything so seriously, my vows, my commitment, and he was—he wasn't."

Reed nodded but didn't comment. A long moment passed, and then he said, "Enough about Andrew and your ex. You came to my hometown to have a good time and forget about the past. Right? So, let's talk about our next date. How about tomorrow at my place, just the two of us and a nice bottle of wine?"

Jessica couldn't help smiling at the blatant invitation. "I don't think so."

"My apartment is right on the beach. We can sit out on the deck and hear the waves crashing on the sand."

"It sounds nice, but no."

"Why not?"

"I told you."

"You're not interested in dating," he parroted. "I assume that means you're not interested in getting married again."

"Definitely not. At least not for a while. I would like Andrew to have a father, but only if it's the right man, one I know we can count on. But as for marriage right now, I don't think so."

"That's great. Because I don't want to get married right now, either. Therefore, I don't see any reason why the two of us can't spend time together. Isn't that why you came here? To loosen up, let your hair down?''

"I was referring to Andrew."

"I think you both could use a little fun in your lives. And I'm an expert at fun."

Jessica chuckled. "And an expert at Frisbee and pizza. Is there no limit to your talents?"

"Why don't you try me and see?"

"Stop, please. You're wasting a lot of great lines on someone who really isn't interested." Jessica tried to put as much honesty as she could into her statement, but deep down she knew she was telling a bald-faced lie. She hadn't been so interested in a man since Theo. Maybe not even him. Theo had been different. He had swept her off her feet with poetry and chocolates, promises of eternal love. She didn't remember laughing with him in the beginning—or in the end.

"You're really denting my ego," Reed complained. "What don't you like about me? My hair? My body? My eyes? My deodorant? What?"

"Nothing," she said with a laugh. "And I think you'll live if you and I don't date. Don't you have someone in your life whom you're seeing now?"

"No." His face darkened as his finger traced a circle on the tabletop. "I was involved with a woman a while back, but that's over now. She moved away, and I'm free as a bird."

"Is she the one who hurt you?"

"Why do you ask that?"

"You mentioned something about liking the wrong person."

"No, it wasn't her. It goes back a lot further than her. She was just moving in a different direction, and there was the big *M* in her future.

"The big *M?*"

"Marriage."

"Right, you don't want to get married."

"No, I don't. But I tell everyone that up front. I don't make any false promises."

"Then why can't you accept the fact that someone doesn't like your game plan?"

He tipped his head in acknowledgement of her point. "It's possible that I can be a little hardheaded, but I don't think that's the reason you don't want to go out with me. You just got out of a bad marriage."

"That's true. But I'm not ruling it out in my future." She smiled. "So ask someone else. You must have dozens of women in a little black book somewhere, probably filed under brunettes, blondes and redheads."

"I don't have any redheads on the list. They've always scared me."

"Why?"

"I'll never tell."

"You can't make a statement like that and then refuse to explain. What's the problem with redheads?"

"They remind me of fire—captivating and dangerous."

"But you fight fires every day."

"And so far I've never gotten burned."

Their eyes connected and suddenly the spark of fun turned into a spark of serious emotion. She took in a breath and held it. His gaze was making her stomach turn somersaults. She wanted to reach out a hand and trace the shadow of beard along his jawline, the fullness of his mouth, his lips.

Thank God, she couldn't move. If she did, she would probably embarrass herself.

"Jess?" Reed's voice was questioning, his blue eyes darkening with intensity.

"What?" she mumbled.

"I'm going to ask you out again."

"I thought you were scared of redheads."

"I am, but I like to live dangerously." He paused. "There's something different about you—about us." He cleared his throat awkwardly. "And that's not a line, just an observation." He pushed back his chair. "I better rescue Andrew from the video games and Wiley from the back seat of my car."

His abrupt departure from the table left her feeling oddly alone. She had been so caught up in their conversation that she hadn't spared the other diners even a thought. Now, she realized that the place had filled up and people were waiting for her table. With a brisk motion, she gathered their trash into a pile and walked over to the wastebasket. Dinner was over, and it was time for things to get back to normal.

Driving home they were all very quiet, and it gave Jessica a chance to regain her composure and her resolve to keep Reed at a distance. By the time they pulled up in front of the house, she was ready to do battle.

"You don't have to get out," she said to Reed. "It's late, and Andrew needs to get to bed."

Reed nodded. "Okay." He reached out and ruffled Andrew's hair. "I had a great time today, buddy. You want to do it again sometime?"

"Yes. If it's okay?" Andrew looked at Jessica for approval, and she gamely twisted her mouth into a smile.

"Of course, but I'm sure Reed is busy at the firehouse."

"I am, but I can make time for my friends. In fact, I'd like to show you around the station sometime."

Andrew's eyes lit up. "Can I sit in the fire truck?"

"I think so."

"And blow the horn? That would be cool."

Andrew and Reed talked back and forth about the station, and Jessica grew increasingly uneasy. She didn't want Reed to play around with Andrew. What if he let him down? Hurt him in some way? Not to mention the fact that any continued involvement with Andrew would mean her involvement as well, which was probably just what Reed wanted.

"I really don't think—" she began, only to be cut off by a sudden flash of anger across Reed's face.

"What's the problem, Jess?"

Andrew also looked at her inquiringly, a pinched frown drawing his brows together.

"I just don't want to take you away from your job."

"Teaching kids about fire prevention is part of my job. How about Monday after school? If we get called out, you can wait around or we can try another day."

"That would be great," Andrew replied. "All right, Mom?"

How could she say no? Andrew was finally coming to life. She couldn't squash his pleasure for her own selfish reasons. "Yes. Thank you for the invitation. It's thoughtful of you."

"Very politely said." Reed nodded approvingly. "You have the most wonderful manners."

Jessica frowned, sensing an implied insult in the compliment. "Thank you, I think."

"Andrew why don't you go on up to the house? I want to ask your mom something."

Before Jessica could protest, Andrew was skipping up the steps with Wiley behind him.

"What?" she demanded.

"Why don't you want me to be friends with Andrew?"

"I don't want you to hurt him."

"Hurt him? I genuinely like the kid, and I want to see him smile. You only get to be young once. It's terrible when you don't have a chance to enjoy it." Reed's words rang out with an edge of bitterness, and suddenly the look in his eyes was more sad than playful.

"I want him to enjoy it, too," Jessica said. "But I also want to protect him."

"Spoken like a true mother. You're a gem, Jess. Andrew is lucky." He paused and then smiled, returning to his usual easygoing manner. "If you want to get in touch with me, my number is in the book."

"I won't need to call you. After our visit to the firehouse on Monday, I think we should just go our separate ways. You say you don't want to hurt Andrew, but don't you see that when you get tired of us and move on to the next woman, Andrew will take it personally. He'll feel rejected just like when his father..."

"When his father did what?"

"I can't go into it."

"All right." Reed drummed his fingers restlessly on the steering wheel. "I hear what you're saying, and I understand. I've never gone out with anyone who had kids. I always steered clear of people with responsibilities, but this is different."

"How so?" she asked in bewilderment.

"I can't explain it." He ran a restless hand through his hair. "Not without sounding stupid or crazy. I just haven't been able to stop thinking about you since I got you out of that damn doghouse, and now that I've spent time with you and Andrew, I don't want to say goodbye." He stared hard into her face. "Let's just take it one day at a time."

She sighed wistfully. "It's tempting. Maybe I feel the same way right now, but I have ties that I can't and won't run away from. You've been honest with me, and I want to be honest with you. We're two very different people—"

"Who are very attracted to each other," Reed finished. "Since we're being so honest, why not get to the heart of the matter?"

She crossed her arms in front of her chest, feeling distinctly uncomfortable with the new thrust of their conversation. "Maybe there's a certain spark," she admitted, "but I came to Solana Beach to be on my own. I have Andrew, and I don't need or want another man in my life to complicate things. I don't know how I can say it any clearer than that."

Reed smiled. "Just tell me you don't like me, Jess. Just say the words, and I won't bother you. Go ahead."

Jessica stared back at him and then opened her mouth, willing the words to come out. Unfortunately, lies had never come easy, and this time it was no different. "I—I—I—"

Reed shook his head knowingly. "That's what I thought. You like me."

Jessica slammed the car door on his mocking words and hoped to God he wasn't right.

Chapter Five

"I'm back." Reed leaned against the doorway and smiled.

Jessica drew her robe more tightly around her body, chilled by the early morning air. "What time is it?"

"Eight-thirty or thereabouts. I've been up since seven. I was thinking about you."

She sent him a troubled look, wishing it was a little later in the day for a conversation that was bound to be disturbing. "I told you last night that I wasn't interested."

"Can I come in anyway?"

"No."

"Please, Jess?"

His wheedling smile made her resolve weaken. "I'm not dressed, and Andrew is still asleep."

"Sounds like a good combination to me." He put his hand up as she attempted to shut the door in his face. "I'm kidding, just *kidding*. Five minutes, that's all I ask."

"What do you want?"

"A little conversation and some help." He pulled up a book and held it in front of her face. "I was doing my homework, and I had a question. I thought you could help me."

She stared at him, an irrepressible urge to smile creeping out along the corners of her mouth. "That is the lamest excuse I have ever heard."

"Can I still come in?"

She held the door open and motioned him inside. "Five minutes. That's it." She led him down the hallway to the kitchen. "Do you want some coffee? I was just putting some on."

"Will I be here long enough to drink it?"

"That depends on your conversation," she retorted, feeling energized by the exchange. Reed made her feel like a worthy opponent, not a cowed victim. Even though he was pushy, he still showed respect, and she liked that. After turning on the coffeemaker, she pulled out a chair at the kitchen table and sat across from him. "Now, what seems to be the problem?"

Reed opened his book and pointed to a series of phrases. "What's this word?"

"*Querida,*" she said. "It means darling or dear."

"I had a feeling it was an important word." His blue eyes twinkled at her. "How about this one?"

"*Amiga.* Girlfriend."

"I knew you could clear things up for me."

She sent him a wry smile. "I thought you were taking this class so you could talk to people during a fire. I don't think those words are going to help."

"Maybe I'll vacation in Mexico." He arched his eyebrows suggestively. "Maybe with you."

"Maybe alone." She got up as the coffeemaker clicked off. "How do you like it? Black or with cream?"

"Black is fine."

She poured the coffee into a mug and handed it to him. "My ex-husband used to drink it with so much cream it was white. I used to wonder why he didn't just have milk."

Reed took a sip of his coffee as he studied her. "It doesn't sound like you had much in common."

"We didn't, but it took me awhile to figure that out." She paused, pouring her own cup of coffee. "I don't want to talk about him. Let's talk about you." She offered him a bright smile as she sat down at the table. "Did you grow up here?"

"Yes, I've lived here all my life, in some bad neighborhoods and some good ones."

"Big family, small family, orphan?" she prodded.

His jaw tightened as he stared down at his coffee. "Big family, then small family, then orphan."

Jessica stared at him in surprise. "I'm sorry. I didn't mean to pry." She paused. "Do you want to tell me what happened?"

"Not really." He softened his sharp answer with a smile. "My parents split up, that's all, but I'm not really an orphan. I have a mother and a sister. Sometimes we're close, sometimes we're not."

"And what are you now?"

"I don't know. I've never been very good at relationships, Jess."

She smiled in understanding. "Neither have I."

"I knew we had something in common."

"That's not enough. In fact, it's probably a detriment. Two bads can't make a good—or something like that."

"Maybe they can. Maybe we just haven't had the right people in our lives." He leaned forward, resting his elbows on the table. "I've never found anyone that I really clicked with."

"What do you mean?"

He shrugged as he searched for the right words. "Being able to talk, feeling a good fit, like when you wear a pair of blue jeans. The new ones are always too tight or too blue or too stiff, but once in a while you put on a pair and they fit—right off the bat, and you know you've been incredibly lucky, because it just doesn't happen that often."

Jessica studied him thoughtfully. "That's true, but finding the right mate is a little more important than buying the wrong pair of jeans. I'm not sure I know how to pick the right person." She took another sip of coffee. "You told me what you don't want, marriage and kids, but what do you want? What's your vision for the future?"

"I don't have one." Reed shook his head at her look of disbelief. "I live for today. I've found that when I set my sights on something, it usually falls through. It's easier if I don't expect anything. If it does come, it's a pleasant surprise. If it doesn't, I'm not disappointed."

It was a telling statement, and one she could completely understand. It was hard to keep dreaming when your dreams had been trampled on. "So, what are you going to do today? Or haven't you thought that far ahead?" she asked, trying to lighten the mood.

He responded in kind. "I'm helping a friend of mine tile his bathroom. His wife gave him the ultimatum. If he doesn't finish today, she's going to a hotel."

Jessica laughed. "Good for her."

"What about you, Jess? Any big plans? Hot dates?"

"No." She stood up and carried her empty cup to the sink. "Andrew and I are going to do a little more exploring, maybe go to the zoo."

"I wish I could go with you. That sounds a lot more fun than tiling. If I hadn't promised Bill..."

Jessica turned to look at him. "Do you always keep your promises?"

He got up and walked over to her, setting his own cup down on the sink. "Always. If I can't keep it, I don't promise."

She crossed her arms in front of her waist, suddenly aware of his closeness and her lack of dress. Theo would be shocked if he could see her now, entertaining a man in her bathrobe. The thought made her smile.

"What's so funny?" Reed asked.

"Just thinking about how far I've come. There was a time in my life when I would not have even come downstairs without taking a shower and doing my hair and makeup. Theo didn't like untidyness, especially on me. It wasn't the right look."

"If Theo didn't like the way you look right now, then he was an idiot. You don't need makeup or any of that other stuff."

Jessica swallowed hard, feeling self-conscious as his gaze raked over her. "I'm a mess." She pushed a clump of hair back behind one ear. "I need to get dressed and check on Andrew."

"I guess that means my five minutes are up."

"You have things to do, and so do I."

He smiled. "Right. I'll see you tomorrow, then. Don't forget—we have a tour of the fire station after school."

"How could I forget? Andrew can't talk about anything else. He's thrilled."

"So am I."

He leaned over and kissed her on the cheek, his lips just brushing the corner of her mouth. It was too sexy to be platonic, but too casual to complain about. She didn't know what to say.

Reed cupped her face with his hands, and she wondered if he was going to take things a step further, but after a long look, he simply said, "Thanks for the coffee."

Then he dropped his hands and walked to the door, slipping into the hall before she could move. She felt like the sun had just gone behind a cloud and the day that had looked so bright seemed a little bit dull.

With a shake of her head, she silently scolded herself. She was doing it again, depending on a man to make her happy. No more. When Andrew got up, they would go out and have a great time. And she would not think about Reed.

The next day Jessica stared at the clock as the school bell rang. In five minutes, Andrew would come bursting through the door, and it would be time to go to the fire station to see Reed. She wasn't sure she was up to it.

Despite her best intentions not to think about the man, he had crept into her subconscious, and she just couldn't shake him loose. Her stomach was tied up in knots, and she had a nagging headache.

Trying to convince herself she was coming down with the flu, she pulled out a desk drawer and took an aspirin. Then she felt her forehead, hoping for a fever. It was normal, and she got even more depressed.

She did not want to feel anything for Reed. She was done with men, done with high emotions, crying and laughing and feeling like she was on top of the world one minute and then landing in a painful heap the next. Love was simply too big a risk.

If she had any sense she'd make up some excuse and cancel their trip to the fire station. But deep down, she knew she couldn't do that. Andrew would be devastated and the disappointment would probably send him right back into his shell. The only thing to do was to go on the tour, thank Reed politely for his time and decline any future invitations.

"I'm ready, Mom," Andrew said, bursting in the door of her classroom with unrepressed excitement.

She smiled at his eager face, silently acknowledging the tingle down her spine. "Is it that time already?"

"Yes. Can we go now? I don't want to be late."

"We have plenty of time. I just hope that they don't get called out before we get there. I don't want you to be disappointed."

"Reed said if he's not there, we can wait until he gets back," Andrew replied.

Jessica put her arms around him and gave him a hug. He stiffened for a moment and then relaxed. When he pulled away, he was still smiling, and she shook her head in wonderment. "I've never seen you so excited. You like Reed don't you?"

"Yeah. Don't you?"

She looked at him and then reluctantly nodded. "I guess I do."

The doors to the fire station were closed when they pulled up to a parking space near the building. Through the windows they could see the front of the red engine, and Andrew let out a whoop of joy, barreling out of the car before Jessica could open the door. She caught up with him at the side door to the station, but he had already rung the bell. She had barely caught her breath when Reed opened the door and said hello.

"Hello." She looked into his eyes and the connection was instant and powerful. If Andrew hadn't been there, she would have been tempted to do something very reckless. But Andrew was there and demanding attention from Reed, who turned to face him somewhat reluctantly.

She felt guilty, hoping Andrew wouldn't realize that Reed was more interested in her than him. Then she felt angry at Reed for putting them both in an uncomfortable situation. Maybe he didn't intend to use her son, but still his friendship was bound to be confusing for Andrew. It was definitely confusing her.

With a worried frown, she watched Reed swing Andrew up into his arms. Now that his attention was focused solely on her son, her tension began to ease. She listened as he told Andrew about the fire station and what they were going to see. There was nothing reluctant in his manner now, no patronizing tone in his voice. In fact, Reed's enthusiasm was contagious, and she was beginning to look forward to their tour.

Their first stop was a big utilitarian but cozy kitchen. Two men were sitting at a long table, sipping coffee and reading the newspaper. She recognized one from her encounter with the doghouse.

"Bill Carlton and Paul Byer," Reed said casually, walking Andrew over to the counter where a plate of cookies waited. "Andrew and Jessica Blake."

Jessica exchanged greetings with the men, feeling a little embarrassed at the curious look in Bill's eyes.

"You're looking in better shape today," Bill said.

"Yes, I'm fine. No side effects."

"At least not for you."

Jessica didn't like the knowing glint in his eyes, so she helped herself to a cookie.

Bill pushed his chair back and stood up. "I hear Reed is going to give you the grand tour."

"And I promised Andrew he could blow the horn," Reed added with a rueful smile. "Sorry guys."

Bill laughed. "Go ahead. Wake up Brownell. He's been napping for over an hour."

"We don't want to be a nuisance," Jessica said quickly. "A quiet walk around will be fine."

"Don't worry, Jess. Everything is okay," Reed said. "Come on, let's go see Big Red."

Their trip through the fire station was long and thorough, but since Reed concentrated on Andrew, Jessica was able to relax and enjoy the tour. She was surprised at how much information Reed imparted, a great deal of it about the problems of fighting fires and the different types of fire they ran into. True to his word, he let Andrew blow the horn and the siren, and even slide partway down the pole. By the time they returned to the kitchen, the other men had left, and they were alone.

Andrew helped himself to more cookies while Jessica sat down at the table. She deliberately picked up the newspaper to distract herself from Reed, but he pulled it away from her. He smiled as he slid down the bench next to her, so close his thigh was brushing against hers. She tried to move away, but she found herself up against the wall and totally out of luck.

"How was school today?" Reed asked.

"Fine," she muttered. "Andrew, why don't you sit down over here?"

"Can I pet the dog?" Andrew asked, pointing to the old dalmatian snoozing in the corner.

"Go ahead. Poppy is very gentle. She's too tired to be anything else and she loves kids," Reed said.

"Poppy? That's a strange name for a dog," Jessica commented.

"Not really. She used to rip up the flowers we planted in the garden every spring. Poppies were her favorite."

"Has she been here long?"

"Over six years. I don't think this place would be the same without her."

"How come fire stations always have dalmatians?" Andrew asked, approaching the dog cautiously.

"A long time ago, the dogs used to run ahead of the horse-drawn fire wagons and clear other animals out of the way. Since then they've been a fireman's best friend," Reed explained.

"Wow, that's cool."

Jessica smiled as Andrew knelt down next to the dog to rub her back.

"I'm going to be on duty until tomorrow night," Reed said, drawing her attention back to him. "But I'm free on Wednesday night."

Jessica looked down at the table. "That's nice."

"I'm thinking about catching a movie and dinner."

"Good for you."

"I hate to go alone."

"So, ask someone out."

"How about you?"

Jessica looked up. "I told you before."

"It's only a movie."

"I would have to get a baby-sitter." As soon as the words came out of her mouth, Jessica realized her mistake.

"Then you would go, if you had a baby-sitter?"

"I didn't say that."

"Yes, you did."

"Well, I don't have a baby-sitter."

"I'll get you one. I have a fourteen-year-old niece, Brandi. She loves kids. I'll call her before you leave."

Jessica immediately shook her head. "I would have to meet her first, and everything is still so new for Andrew here. What if something happened while we were gone?"

"Brandi knows how to call 911. She has a fireman for an uncle. She even knows CPR. I think you're running out of excuses. Hey, Andrew. What do you think of your mom and I going out to a movie and dinner together?"

Andrew shrugged, more intent on petting the dog than getting involved in their argument.

Jessica frowned at Reed. "I'm not going. You are not going to railroad me into a date."

"I was just trying to make it easy on you."

"Let me run my own life, okay?" She jerked to her feet. "We have to go now."

"Jess, wait." Reed stood up, putting a hand on her arm to stop her from leaving. "I'm sorry. I know I'm a little pushy, but every time I see you I get the feeling it's going to be the last time." He tried to laugh, but it fell short, creating a tense silence between them.

Jessica stared at him uncertainly, her resolve wavering at the persuasive tone of his voice, the sincerity of his words. She wanted to be with him. But she wasn't ready. It was too soon. Still, it was tempting to let herself be a woman again, not just a mother, to feel a man's arms around her, see desire and want in his eyes.

"Come to any conclusions?" Reed questioned.

Jessica shook her head. "Unfortunately no."

"I don't know what's going to happen between us, but I think we should find out."

"I'd rather not risk it," Jessica whispered, unable to keep the fear from creeping into her voice. "I want to say yes—but I can't. Please, leave it alone."

"I wish I could. I told myself to just give you this tour and then say goodbye—but I can't do it."

Before Jessica could reply a series of bells pealed through the firehouse, and Reed's manner immediately turned serious. Running feet could be heard coming from every direction as orders were barked out by the captain. The lighthearted man turned into a grim-faced warrior before her eyes, and the transformation was startling.

"I've got to go. We'll talk later."

"Of course," Jessica answered.

Reed headed out of the kitchen with a casual salute to Andrew, and Jessica and Andrew huddled together, watching as the men went to their posts on the engine. Within seconds the truck pulled out of the station, sirens blaring.

"I wish I could go with them," Andrew said. "Do you think Reed will be all right?"

The question echoed through her own mind, and she realized how quickly she had come to care for Reed. "I'm sure he will be," she said. "We better go home. There's no telling how long they'll be gone."

"Can we come back?"

"Maybe sometime. We'll see."

"Are you going to go to the movies with him?"

Jessica sighed and ruffled his hair with her fingers. "I don't know. What do you think?"

"You and Daddy never went to the movies."

"That's true. Your father didn't care much for them."

"I like the movies," Andrew said with a touch of defiance in his voice.

"So do I." Jessica smiled as their eyes met. It was the first time in a long time that she felt like they were on the same side. She reached for his hand and he allowed her to hold it.

Chapter Six

"I can't believe you asked her out." Bill sat in the seat across from Reed as the engine hurtled through the city streets. "You sure do like to live dangerously. Not that she isn't good-looking, but she's got a kid."

Reed offered him a brief smile. "I like Andrew. He needs someone to show him how to have a good time."

"Someone like you?"

"Maybe."

Bill shook his head. "I can't believe what I'm hearing. You're getting involved with a woman who has a child? She's probably looking for a father for her son, a long-term commitment."

"No, she's not interested in getting married again."

"That's what she says now. What happens if that changes?"

"I'll worry about it then. What is it with you and Jessica? Don't we have enough problems today? Do we have to worry about what may never happen?"

Reed looked out the window as they turned into the industrial part of town, his grim expression deepening as the thick smell of smoke surrounded them. Sirens were blaring from the other engines converging on the scene, and with silent efficiency the two men adjusted their coats and hats.

"These old buildings go up like firecrackers," Bill said. "No up-to-date sprinkler systems, nothing. Too bad nobody worried about that yesterday, huh?"

Reed sent him a quelling look, and then the engine slammed to a halt. They jumped down to the ground, their past conversation forgotten as they waited for instructions from the captain.

"We've got one still missing, a teenage girl visiting her father. She was last seen on the third floor," the captain said.

"Please, you have to get my daughter out," a man implored from nearby. "You can't leave her in there to die."

A policeman stepped up to move the distraught man back behind the lines, but Reed could still hear his anguished pleas.

"He's right," Reed said, staring hard at the captain.

The captain nodded. "Do it now." He dropped his voice down to a harsh mutter. "But be careful, I don't want three victims instead of one."

Reed pulled his face mask down and ran into the building. Bill followed at his heels. The flames had engulfed the south end of the building and most of the second floor. The old, worn beams were lighting with every spark, threatening to crash down on them at any second. Bill put a hand on his shoulder as he started for the stairs.

"It's too late. We won't have a chance."

"There's a kid up there. I'm going," Reed said grimly. "You stay here. You've got a wife to think about."

"And let you go up there alone? The hell I will."

Reed ran up the stairs, hopping over a tiny flicker of flames creeping along the edge of the carpet. He had just reached the second-floor landing when an explosion rocked the building. He paused for a moment, waiting for the ceiling to crash down on his head. Thankfully, it held.

Bill shook his head in despair. "I'll take this side. Hurry."

Reed nodded and moved down the opposite hallway as quickly as he could, knowing that time was the enemy. A few seconds, and it would be impossible to save anyone including themselves.

He headed down the hall where the fire was hotter and the rooms were already beginning to break apart. A low moan made him pause, and he waited, wondering if the fire was mimicking the sound of a human in pain.

The groan came again, and he ran toward the desk. A young woman was lying on her back, blood flowing through a cut on her forehead, a heavy picture from the wall lying next to her. Her blond hair was spread out in a semicircle around her head and the innocence of her face sent a rocketing image through his mind.

She looked just like Hayley, the night he had found her on the bathroom floor. He knew he should pick her up, get her out, but his muscles were frozen. He couldn't move. He hadn't been able to rescue his sister, and now he wasn't going to be able to rescue this young girl.

"Reed. This whole place is going." Bill shouted the words, entering the room with a rapid, nervous stride. "You found her. Thank God. Is she alive?" Bill waited, and when there was no reply, he pulled off his mask and put it on the girl.

At the motion, Reed came to his senses and took off his own mask and handed it to Bill. "I'll take her down. Wear mine."

"I don't need it."

"Just do it," Reed commanded, swinging the girl up into his arms.

They ran down the hallway toward the stairs, but when they got there, it was too late. There was no way down.

The evening news was filled with the story of the warehouse fire, and Jessica was in the middle of fixing dinner when she heard the report that two firemen had gone inside to rescue a missing woman.

The potato peeler fell with a clatter against the Formica countertop, and she reached one hand up to steady her heart. Andrew paused in the middle of doing his homework. One look at his mother's worried face sent his gaze flying to the television.

"Do you think it's Reed?" he asked.

"I don't know. It looks like there are a lot of trucks there." It didn't have to be Reed. There were dozens of fire fighters on the scene. Anyone could have risked his life to run into a burning building.

The reporter echoed her thoughts, adding that stations throughout San Diego and Solana Beach were sending forces to fight the fire which was now threatening to jump to the next building.

The uneasy feeling in the pit of her stomach grew stronger as she watched in fearful fascination. Through the power of the camera lens, she could almost feel the heat, smell the smoke and the fear. What if Reed was in that burning building? Would he be all right?

"Where is he?" she muttered, her gaze raking the corners of the television, hoping that his grinning face would be captured even for a split second so that she could regain her breath.

"He'll be all right, Mom," Andrew said. "He's tough, and he knows just what to."

"I know he is, honey."

The reporter's voice suddenly roared with excitement, and the camera panned over to the far edge of the building where a fireman was barreling down the outside fire escape, a body draped over his shoulder. Another fire fighter was following them. It seemed to take an endless amount of time for them to reach the ground but finally they were there, and a group of paramedics took the victim and began to work on the girl.

The fireman had his back to the camera, but Jessica knew instinctively that it was Reed. There was something in his aggressive stance, the breadth of his shoulders that was already familiar to her.

The camera crew swept in closer, trying to get a picture of the victim and the rescuer. The reporter called out for the fireman, and Jessica watched as he slowly turned around.

"It's Reed," Andrew said excitedly. "He did it. He saved that girl."

Jessica nodded; she couldn't speak. Her throat tightened with a knot of emotion growing so large she could barely swallow. Reed's face was black from the soot and sweat was pouring off his forehead, but his bright blue eyes shone out like a beacon in the darkness and when he smiled briefly into the camera, she felt like he had kissed her.

Another rush of emotion filled her, bringing moisture to her eyes, and she turned around, hiding her face from Andrew. He wouldn't understand why she felt like crying. She didn't understand it herself. How had she come to care for a man so fast? She had tried to lock away her emotions. But it hadn't worked; somehow he had sneaked into her life, into her heart, and it had only been a few days. How would she feel after another week? Another month?

She took in a deep breath and slowly let it out, repeating the motion again and again, until a sense of calm seeped into her tight muscles. She tried to tell herself that anyone would be worried about a friend in danger, but deep down she knew she was in trouble—big trouble.

Reed stared at the phone. It was one o'clock in the morning, and Jessica would be asleep. If he called, he would probably wake up Andrew. Still, his fingers hovered over the receiver. Eight hours of fighting an intense fire had left him thirsty for something cool and refreshing, a calming voice, Jessica's voice.

His fingers punched out the buttons, ignoring the command from his brain to stop. He was getting involved, and it was a big mistake. He would only hurt her, or she would hurt him. Somewhere, somebody would get hurt.

He closed his eyes, his fingers clenching the receiver to his ear as he listened for the ring. He felt like a kid again, calling a girl for the first time, hoping she would answer, praying she wouldn't, because then he'd have to talk and put himself on the line. No one had ever known what he'd gone through, the insecurity his brash manner had always covered up. He was the tough kid, the cool guy who could get any girl he wanted—except the right one. He was still looking for her.

Jessica would probably be furious at the call. She didn't even want to go out with him, much less have him interrupt her sleep. He started to set the phone down, when he heard her voice.

"Hello," she said. "Hello. Is anyone there?"

He heard the sudden worry in her voice, and he knew he had to say something. "Hi, Jess, it's me."

There was a long pause. "Reed? Are you all right?"

"Sure, why wouldn't I be?"

"I heard about how bad the fire was."

"It's out now. I didn't realize how late it was. You were probably asleep."

"Yes."

He played with the phone cord and tried to think of something to say. He wanted to tell her about the girl he'd found, about the way he'd felt, but it was too long a story to begin over the phone. "I'm sorry. I'll let you get back to bed."

"Wait," Jessica said. "Are you sure you're okay? You sound a little funny."

"I'm tired. It's been a long day, but I feel too keyed up to sleep. I don't know why I called."

"I'm glad you did," she admitted. "I was worried about you. I've never known a fireman before. I guess I'd forgotten what kind of danger you get into."

"Most of the time I'm just rescuing women out of doghouses, but once in a while, we get some action, like today."

"Do you ever get scared out there?"

"Me? Are you kidding?"

She chuckled softly, and he smiled at the sound. He had always been able to make people laugh, one of his few strengths, and he was happy to see it was still working. Jessica needed to laugh more, to enjoy life, and he wanted to be the one to show her how to do that.

"You don't have to put on a macho act for me," Jessica continued. "I already know you have a soft spot for kids and dogs."

"And redheads," he murmured.

"What if I told you my hair color came out of a bottle?"

"I'd say you were lying, and I'd know right away, because you couldn't lie to save your life." He settled himself more comfortably in his chair. "I've never known anyone like you, Jess. Honest, straightforward, not to mention gorgeous."

Jessica laughed nervously. "I'm a regular Girl Scout, Reed. That's why I don't know what to say when you start flirting with me, and I wish you'd stop."

"I'm not flirting, just telling it like it is. I know I woke you up, but I wanted to hear your voice. It's cool and refreshing like a mountain stream after a long hot hike, and that's what I feel like I've been doing today."

"Do you like being a fireman?"

The unexpected question made him pause. "No one has ever asked me that before. They just assume I do."

"Probably because you seem so well-suited to the job."

"I do like it. The danger and the excitement are part of the reason why, but it feels good to be in a position to help people, maybe even save them from themselves—not that I'm always successful." He cleared his throat, feeling a deep sense of emotion tightening his vocal cords.

"Do you ever get lonely, Reed?"

He sucked in his breath at the question. It would be easy to make a joke, but it was the middle of the night and he was alone. "Yeah, every now and then."

"So do I. I've never told that to anyone." She uttered a short laugh. "I don't know why I told you."

"I better hang up now," Reed said, twisting the cord into a tight knot. "It's late."

"I'm glad you called."

"Really?"

"Yes," she said softly. "It feels good to be needed. I haven't felt this way in a long time."

Her voice broke and she hung up, leaving the sound of a dial tone buzzing in his ear, and the truth ringing through his soul. He was starting to need her, too, and he didn't like the feeling—not one little bit.

Jessica pulled the covers up to her chin and stared at the ceiling. She was wide awake and tomorrow she would be exhausted, but for the moment she felt invigorated and excited like something wonderful was about to happen.

Of course, she was making too much out of a simple phone call. But she couldn't remember the last time a man had called her just to talk, to hear the sound of her voice, to be reassured by her presence. Theo had never confided in her, never shared his problems or his joys.

It was foolish to compare the two men. They were as different as night and day, steak and hamburger. Maybe that was a good sign. Maybe she was finally on the right track.

Jessica's excitement dimmed during the next two days as she went about her usual schedule. She had expected to hear from Reed again, but the phone remained silent, and she was too much of a coward to call him. The long hours without contact only reinforced her doubts and insecurities and by the time Wednesday afternoon rolled around, she had pretty much convinced herself that whatever was happening between them was over.

The only bright spot was Andrew's blossoming mood. On the ride home from school, he bubbled over with enthusiasm about his school day. Being friends with the local hero had helped him mix with the other children. Now that the ice was broken, she had a feeling Andrew was well on his way to being accepted by his classmates.

While Andrew was chattering, her thoughts turned to Juanita, the child in her class whose sadness seemed to grow with each passing day. It was getting to the point where the little girl barely spent fifteen minutes without bursting into tears, and efforts to reach Juanita's parents had been futile. She had finally asked Donna for Juanita's address when the little girl failed to show up for school. She had a bad feeling, and she wanted to go by Juanita's house and make sure the little girl was okay.

To her surprise, the one-story house on a quiet residential street was beautifully tended, which was at odds with Juanita's often bedraggled appearance. With an admonition for Andrew to wait in the car, she walked up to the door and rang the bell.

A tall blond woman opened the door, a toddler about three years old hanging around her leg. "Yes, can I help you?"

Jessica looked at her uncertainly. "I'm looking for Juanita Guerrero."

"There's no one here by that name."

"This is 127 Bailey Drive."

"Last time I looked." The toddler began to wail and the woman shrugged her shoulders. "I have to go."

"Wait. I'm looking for two little girls, Juanita and Rosa. They speak Spanish, and they're supposed to live on this street."

"Sorry, but I know all the kids in the neighborhood, and they don't live here."

The woman shut the door in her face, and Jessica walked slowly back to her car.

"Did you find them, Mom?" Andrew asked.

"No. They don't live here."

"Are we going somewhere else?"

Jessica shook her head. "I don't know where else to go. No one answers their phone, and this isn't their house. Something's going on, and I don't like it." She slid into the front seat and turned her key in the ignition.

"Do you think we're going to see Reed again?"

Andrew's innocent question made her flood the engine with gas, and she quickly pulled her foot off the accelerator. "Why do you ask that?"

"I want to hear about the fire. Aren't you going to the movies with him tonight?"

"No."

"But he asked you to."

"That was on Monday, and I haven't heard from him since. He's probably busy or working."

"Or maybe he found a new friend," Andrew said, his bright mood fading rapidly. "Can we go home now? I want to do my homework."

Jessica pulled the car into the street, wishing she could cheer Andrew up, but if the truth be told, she felt a little depressed herself. They were both silent on the drive home, but the sight of a Jeep Wrangler in front of their house abruptly changed their moods.

Andrew barely waited for the car to stop before hurtling his small body onto the driveway and running over to Reed, who was sitting casually on the front steps. Jessica followed more slowly, hoping to get her emotions under control before she saw him again.

"Hi," he said simply, the look in his eyes welcoming the sight of her.

She drank it in like a long cool drink on a hot day. "Are you okay?"

"Me? I'm terrific."

"We saw you on television," Andrew said. "When you rescued that girl. It was awesome."

"Right. I forgot the television cameras were there. How did I look? Did they get my good side?" He swung his jaw around from one side to the other.

"Actually you were covered in soot," Jessica replied.

"Great. My one shot at fame, and I needed a shower."

"It was cool," Andrew said, ignoring their teasing comments. "We could see the flames coming out of the building and when the glass window blew out, that was really bad."

"It was quite a fire," Reed agreed. "Thankfully, we don't get too many of those around here."

"I want to be a fireman when I grow up."

Reed smiled at Andrew. "We could use more good men." He paused. "I'm kind of tired of talking about the fire, though. I was hoping I could steal your mom away for a while." He turned to Jessica. "My niece can baby-sit."

Jessica hesitated. "I just went to the grocery store, and I should get dinner going for Andrew."

"Won't it keep?"

"Probably, but—"

"Is that okay with you, Andrew? We won't be gone long, and maybe when we get back you and I can play one of your computer games." He looked up at Jessica as he finished speaking. "I know I'm pushing, but I need to talk to you."

"All right."

"You're saying yes?"

"Yes. As long as it's an early night."

"Can't I come, too?" Andrew asked. "I want to hear about the fire."

"I'll tell you all about it when we get back. I promise."

Andrew regarded him seriously. "Are you sure?"

"When I make a promise, I keep it." Reed patted him on the back. "Besides, you'll like Brandi. She's a lot of fun. If it's all settled, I'll go pick her up. Will that give you enough time?"

Jessica nodded. "I think so."

Reed poked a finger at the top button on her white blouse. "Put on some tight jeans, wear tennis shoes, and see if you can find a top that doesn't doesn't make you look like a nun. I wouldn't want to hurt my reputation."

"I dress for myself these days, thank you. And if you don't want me the way I am, you can always ask someone else."

"I don't want anyone else," he said with a wheedling smile. "I just want more—of you."

Chapter Seven

It was half past four when Jessica slid into the front seat of Reed's Wrangler, and although the days were getting shorter as they headed into October, it was still warm and sunny. She had agonized over what to wear, not wanting to give in to Reed's demand but at the same time wanting to look good for him. She had settled on a pair of new blue jeans that weren't tight, but did fit her figure, and a light blue, short-sleeved T-shirt with a scoop neckline and no buttons.

She liked the feel of the sun on her bare arms. In Boston, everything had been so sterile because of the cold weather and her ex-husband's phobia of germs. Here in California, she had begun to get in touch with the sensual part of her nature. She liked the sun beating down on her head, the smell of jasmine in the air, the sound of the crickets at nighttime. Sure there was smog and all the other negatives, but with the beach...

They turned the corner then, and she looked out over the sparkling blue water reflecting the setting sun. Maybe it was Reed, maybe it was just her mood, but she had a feeling that on a gorgeous night like this, heaven couldn't be too far away.

"Aren't you curious as to where we're going?" Reed asked.

"No. I'm sure it will be perfect. You're probably an expert on restaurants."

"In this neck of the woods, definitely." He smiled at her, long and tender. "It's good to see you."

A shiver ran through her body at the serious turn of his words. "It has only been a couple of days."

"Seems like longer."

He drove in silence for a while, winding the car along the edge of the ocean. Jessica was content to let the breeze blow through her hair and enjoy the view. It was a companionable silence, and one that probably wouldn't last if she let herself think about anything but the moment.

Finally, Reed turned into a parking lot on a bluff overlooking the beach. Jessica looked at him inquiringly. There were a few cars and a small building for rest rooms but no restaurant in sight.

"Why are we stopping?"

"Because we've arrived." He opened the car door and got out, waiting for her to join him.

"I don't see any restaurants," she said, as she walked around to his side of the car.

His eyes twinkled down at her. "That's because you're not using your imagination. Picture a perfect spot overlooking the water." He waved his hand for effect.

"Okay, I'm picturing it. What else?"

"A white tablecloth, a very fine bottle of wine."

"Candles?"

"No, sorry, no candles."

"Okay, I can live without them."

"Good."

"But what are we eating?"

He waved a finger at her in reproach. "The chef's special, of course."

"Is it any good?"

"Use your imagination."

"I am," Jessica said dryly. "And I still can't conjure up a restaurant out here. Maybe we better use your imagination."

Reed put a casual arm around her shoulders and led her to the back of the car where he opened the rear door. Inside was a worn sports bag, a pair of cleats, two baseball bats, a backpack and two pairs of roller skates. Reed reached in and grabbed one pair of skates.

"These are for you. They're roller blades."

"They're what?"

"Roller blades. It's the new rage. They're better than roller skates, because you can really maneuver on the turns. Hockey players use them for training off the ice."

Jessica looked at him in bewilderment. "What do they have to do with me?"

"You need to wear them to get where we're going."

"I thought we were going to dinner."

"We are, but I could use a little exercise first—to work up an appetite."

"I'm already hungry."

Reed made a disapproving face. "When was the last time you got out and exercised?"

"I run after five-year-olds all day long."

"That's not the same thing." He folded his arms across his chest and waited. "Of course if you don't want to do it, I'll understand. We'll just get in the car and drive to some nice, boring restaurant and order some bland chicken dish."

Jessica couldn't help laughing. "You make it sound like torture."

"I just think my idea is better."

Jessica looked down at the skates doubtfully. "I'm not sure I can even stand up in those."

"Didn't you roller skate as a child?"

"Yes, but that was a long time ago. I might fall down. In fact, I'm pretty sure of it."

"I'll hold you up, don't worry. You're going to love this."

"Okay. I'll give it a try, as long as you promise not to laugh."

"Would I do that?" Reed led her over to the cement wall overlooking the beach. "Sit here and I'll help you get laced up."

Once Jessica had her skates on, she tried to stand up and felt the earth shoot out from under her. She hadn't even gotten fully upright before she landed hard on her bottom.

Reed started to laugh.

"You promised."

"Sorry, but you weren't even moving."

"And I don't think I will be any time soon."

Reed pulled her up with two hands and then slid his arms around her waist, pulling her right up against his body. "How's that?" he asked.

With the breath of his words fanning her cheek in a delightful manner, Jessica could only struggle to get out one coherent word. "Fine."

His eyes twinkled mischievously, as he pulled her even closer, bringing her legs between his, pulling her hips into the cradle of his pelvis. "Maybe we won't skate after all."

"You're not playing fair," Jessica replied. "If I pull away, I'm going to fall right on my fanny again."

"So don't pull away." His eyes darkened with intent, and he lowered his head, brushing her mouth gently with his. Jessica couldn't help responding to the tender pressure. His mouth was so warm, the kiss so sweet. He was passionate but not overwhelming. She could have pulled away, but she didn't want to. She wanted to get closer.

She wrapped her arms around his neck, tilting her head to deepen the kiss. Her senses were focused only on the moment, his lips against hers, his chest against her breasts, and his hand creeping up from her waist to run through the strands of her hair.

When Reed finally lifted his head, his grip around her waist loosened, and Jessica was so caught up in her emotions that her feet started to slide before she remembered she was standing on roller blades. Reed grabbed her at the last second, pulling her back into his arms with a laugh.

"If I'd known you kissed like that, I certainly wouldn't have done it with you on roller blades."

"Me, what about you?" she said, feeling slightly embarrassed by her passionate response.

"I just aim to please."

"If that's the case, maybe you could please me by skipping the skating portion of our evening. I don't think I can do it."

"Yes, you can. Here, sit down for a moment, and let me get my own skates on."

Jessica sat down on the bench and held on tight while he laced up his skates. In a way, she was grateful for the short break. She needed to regain her poise, or at least some control over the situation. But with a look down at her skates, she realized that was a hopeless thought.

"Ready?" Reed asked. "Wait a second. I almost forgot." He skated easily over to the back of his car and pulled out the backpack and the sports bag. Then he closed the trunk, whirling around with an expertise that made her frown.

"Are you sure you don't want to drive to this place?" she asked.

"That would be safe but not particularly exciting."

"That's me, safe and secure."

Reed shook his head. "No, I think that was the old Jessica, not the new Jess."

"We're one and the same."

"Take this."

Jessica took the backpack reluctantly. "It better not have smelly socks in it."

"You never know with me."

"I'm beginning to realize that." Jessica put her arms through the backpack so that it was situated comfortably on her back. It wasn't heavy, just bulky. "Now what?"

"Now, we skate to our restaurant of course." He put a hand on her chin and tilted up her face so she was looking directly into his eyes. "Think of this as an adventure, a moment in time. You don't have any worries, any problems or any responsibilities. Not tonight. It's just you and me, baby."

Jessica smiled back at him, irresistibly pulled in by his charm. It was fun to banter and flirt. It had been so long since she had allowed herself to say what she wanted to say, to do what she felt like doing. "Lead on, Captain, but if you're walking the plank, don't expect me to jump. I do have a mind of my own, even though it seems to be out to lunch at the moment."

"You're going to enjoy this. Just remember that you're in control of the skates, not the other way around."

"Maybe you should tell them that," Jessica replied, pointing down at her skates.

"When you stand up, keep your weight forward. We'll start out slow and gradually go faster. You want to push off with the skate and glide." Reed demonstrated with an agility that only emphasized the difference between them. "If you feel like we're going too fast, let me know, and I'll stop."

"You promise?"

"Trust me," Reed said.

"I'd like to, believe me." She paused. "But I'm not sure what you think is good for me and what I think is good for me are one and the same."

Reed didn't respond. He simply held out his hands and helped her to her feet.

Jessica concentrated on standing upright and after a moment, she felt a little steadier.

"Ready to move now?" Reed asked.

"As I'll ever be."

Reed stood behind her and placed both hands on her waist so that he could keep her upright. "Okay, just let yourself glide for a minute. Push off gently."

Jessica did as she was told and was surprised she was still standing. She took a few more tentative steps and then pushed off. True to his word, Reed kept his hands on her waist murmuring encouragement.

"Keep gliding," he instructed. "Push off with your right and then your left. That's it. You're getting the hang of this."

"It's coming back to me, slowly." Jessica grew more confident with each step and pretty soon they were actually starting to move at a pace a little faster than a snail's.

"Once you feel comfortable, I'm going to come around to the side and take your hand."

"I don't think I'm ready."

"You're doing fine. Here I go."

Jessica experienced a sudden panic when his hands left her waist, and she stumbled, but he grabbed her hand and kept her steady. He smiled over at her. "You're a natural."

"Hardly that," she murmured, feeling pleased by the compliment.

"We're going to skate down this path for awhile, and when you stop worrying about your feet, you can take a look out at the ocean. The sun will be setting in a few minutes."

Jessica didn't think she'd be able to look at anything but the ground, but as they moved down the path away from the parking lot, she began to relax a little. Reed wasn't going to let her fall and she was actually starting to enjoy herself

They were quiet as they moved along the bluff overlooking the water. It was a spectacular beach, and Jessica couldn't fault Reed on the beauty of the scene. The pristine path eventually turned into a rockier road, and Jessica became concerned about the bumps and potholes.

"Maybe we should turn back," she suggested.

"No, we're almost there."

"Almost where?"

"To our restaurant." Reed pulled her off the cement into the grass, and she looked at him in surprise. "We have to walk the rest of the way," he admitted. "I think you can manage in the skates."

"Since my shoes are in your car, I certainly hope so."

Reed laughed. "I like your style, Jess. When I first met you, I didn't know what to make of you. You had more starch in you than my shirts when they come back from the cleaners."

"I doubt that. At our first meeting, my butt was hanging out of a doghouse."

"True, but that night you gave me such a cold shoulder, I thought I'd catch pneumonia."

"I wasn't that bad."

"Yes, you were. You had 'hands off' written all over you."

"I hope I still do," she said.

"The ink is fading fast, and I'm glad we're getting to know each other now. You're not as uptight as the clothes you wear."

"I don't know what I am anymore," Jessica replied. "I think I'm still finding out."

Reed nodded and took her hand. "Watch your step. It gets rocky through this part."

He led her through a bushy, overgrown area and even down a slight incline that they managed wobbling and laughing. Finally, they reached a grassy plateau that overlooked the water.

"Your table, madame." Reed motioned for her to sit down and she did so, sliding her legs out from under her. Then he reached into the paper bag and pulled out a white tablecloth and spread it over the dirt. "Now your turn."

"Me?"

"Open the bag."

Jessica pulled the backpack off her shoulders and unzipped it. She gasped aloud at the contents. She didn't know what she had been expecting, probably some turkey sandwiches from the deli, but inside was a bottle of wine and two glasses, a plastic container of rice salad, fried chicken and some French bread. "This looks wonderful. Did you do all this yourself?"

"That's my secret."

"Even if you didn't, I like the thought. Can I take my skates off now?"

"Sure, go ahead."

Jessica undid the laces and slipped the skates off her feet. Then she went to work unpacking the backpack. While Reed opened the wine, she picked up a chicken wing to nibble on and stared out at the view. It was truly magnificent. She felt a rush of emotion that she couldn't explain, and blinked back a sudden moisture behind her eyes.

Reed filled the glasses and handed her one. Then he hesitated. "A toast would probably be good right about now."

Jessica nodded. "That would be nice."

"Do you want to make it?" he asked hopefully.

"No way. This is your imagination, remember."

"Okay." He paused, thinking for a long moment. "Here's to taking chances and no regrets."

Jessica took a sip of her wine, wondering if she could really drink to such a toast. But Reed was right. Tonight was an adventure, and she knew no matter what happened between them she wouldn't regret this romantic picnic.

"Do you ever have regrets about the things you've done?" she asked thoughtfully.

Reed stared out at the water and smiled. "I'm sorry that I never became a professional surfer. I would have loved traveling the world, hitting the best beaches, the biggest, most dangerous waves. I still go out now when I get a chance, but it's not the same."

"Why didn't you become a surfer? It sounds like your dream job."

"Believe me, I thought about it. But in the end, I decided fighting fires was a little more practical."

"Practical, you?"

"I do have to eat, and I have a pretty good appetite. Fighting fires satisfies the need in me for excitement, at least most of the time."

Jessica shook her head in amazement. "A fireman that surfs, interesting combination. It must be the California influence in your life."

"Probably."

"What else, Mr. McAllister? What else do you regret?"

A solemn expression crossed his face, and he took a long sip of his wine. Then he set the glass down and reclined, resting on his elbows. "I think the things we regret most in life are the things we don't do. Maybe that's why I take chances. I want to try everything. I want to really live."

"Does everyone in your family have such a streak of adventure?"

"Only the males. My dad left when I was twelve to work in the pits for a race car driver. He never came back."

"I'm sorry. That must have been difficult for you and your mother."

"Yeah, but Mom was the opposite of Dad. No big dreams for her. She got a job as a waitress at the downtown coffee shop. That was twenty years ago, and she's still there."

"Maybe she likes it."

"I guess she does."

"But you don't approve."

"I think she's just too scared to quit. It was hard when my dad left. There was no money, so we all got jobs. I had a paper route and took care of my younger sister, Hayley, after school."

"Sounds like you were a very responsible little boy."

"No," he said, his voice filled with a sudden harshness. "I wasn't good at taking care of other people. A chip off the old block, I guess. My dad put his dreams ahead of everyone else, and it made our lives a living hell."

Jessica set her wine down and stretched out next to him, studying the serious lines in his face. "Why do you say that? What happened?"

"You don't want to hear all this."

"Yes, I do. I want to understand you, get to know you better."

"Hey, there's nothing to understand." He forced a smile. "I'm a carefree, happy-go-lucky guy now. And we have the world at our feet.'' He sat up and stretched his arms out wide as if he were embracing the ocean. Then he turned to her, all trace of his earlier tension gone. ''Not to mention the fact that I have a gorgeous redhead at my side who finally agreed to go out with me.''

''It didn't take you that long to convince me,'' Jessica said dryly. ''And you're changing the subject.''

''That's because I'm hungry and talking about my family always makes me lose my appetite. You don't want to waste this wonderful picnic, do you?''

''No, but sometime I'm going to ask you again.''

''It's not that big a deal, Jess, really.'' He reached over and opened the rice salad, spooning a serving onto a plate. ''Now, it's your turn. What do you regret?''

''Me?'' Jessica sat up, chewing thoughtfully on her chicken wing for a long moment. ''I don't know where to start. I have a lot of regrets.''

''Like what?''

''Marrying too young. Listening too much to my parents and my husband, not thinking for myself.''

''What actually happened with your husband? Irreconcilable differences as they say in divorce court?''

Jessica tossed the chicken wing down on her plate and folded her knees against her chest, closing her arms around them. ''Yes, but it really starts with my parents. My father is a dean at a private college in Massachusetts, and I was thrust into academics with a vengeance. I couldn't participate in any after-school activity unless it had some educational value.''

''You must be one smart lady.''

''No, I was pretty dumb to put up with it all. Anyway, I went to the college where my father was the dean and that's where I met Theo. He was in his third year as a teacher of English, and I was totally enraptured. I was a junior then and I had heard about him since I was a freshman. He's really very handsome.''

"Great," Reed said dryly. "Go on."

"I was flattered when Theo started to call on me in class, and when he invited me out for coffee one afternoon, I fell head over heels. He was just the kind of man my parents had encouraged me to look for. We had a whirlwind romance and got married that summer in between semesters.''

"Wait, let me guess." Reed held up a hand, making her pause. "He married you to impress your father and to make a valuable connection."

Jessica frowned. "Okay, so it's not an original problem, but it was news to me. I was in love with this man. I adored him with the infatuation of a twenty-one-year-old girl. I married him and put his needs first. I had a child right away because he wanted a son, and I worked my schooling in around his schedule.'' She paused and held out her empty wineglass. "Can I have a refill?''

Reed reached out and poured her some wine. "You don't have to talk about this if you don't want to.''

"It's okay. You're pretty easy to talk to. I never get the feeling that you're judging me.''

"I don't judge anyone. I don't have the right. Now go on, why did you get divorced?''

"Because I found out he was unfaithful to me, not once but dozens of times, usually with the young women in his classes. The first time I thought it was just an aberration, that it was something I had done to make him look elsewhere, and everything he said seemed to confirm that.''

"Nice guy."

"He was very manipulative and mean-spirited. I know that now, but back then I was afraid to divorce him. I had a son to think about, and I wasn't sure I could make it on my own. Theo told me over and over again that I would be lost without him. Like a fool I believed him. And my parents weren't any help. They liked Theo. Even when I mentioned our problems, they thought it was my imagination. The turning point was Andrew. When Theo sent him to that academy, something inside me snapped, and I knew I had to get us both out. So, here I am."

"Here you are," Reed echoed. "For what it's worth, I think you made the right choice, not the safe one. It was a risk, and you took it. We have more in common than you think."

"I don't know about that. My move here was completely out of character, and it took an extraordinary circumstance to make me leave. Other women would have cut and run a long time ago, but I was chicken."

Reed handed her a chicken wing in reply, and she started to laugh. "Then, you better eat this," he said.

"You're good for me, Reed. And you're good for Andrew. The thing I want most in my life is to see him turn into a happy, healthy, normal little boy, maybe a few quirks, but I want him to be able to talk to me, to trust me. And I want him to enjoy life the way it should be enjoyed."

"All you have to do is invite me over more often. I can loosen the kid up for you."

"I know you can. I already said you were good for us—at least in that way." She set her food down on the tablecloth and stared at him. His face was lit by the setting sun, strong and tan with lines of character and laughter edging his eyes. She leaned forward intently. "The question is, are we good for you?"

Chapter Eight

Reed didn't smile at her question. He just stared back at her in a solemn way that was disconcerting. After a moment, he reached out a hand and ran it down the length of one copper strand of hair. Then his hand crept around to the back of her neck, and he pulled her closer, shifting until their faces were just inches apart.

Jessica's heart started to race, and she couldn't have pulled away if her life depended on it. His other hand reached out to caress her cheek, trailing down to trace the line of her mouth.

"I think we could be very good together," he muttered.

And then his mouth met hers for the second time that evening. There wasn't any hesitancy this time, just a pure, deep longing to be together. They shifted positions until Jessica was lying down on her back in the soft grass and Reed was exploring her mouth with a thoroughness that drove everything else from her mind.

She ran her hands through the curls at the base of his neck and down and around the sculpted muscles of his back. He was a strong man. She could feel his power, but despite the passion there was a tenderness in his embrace that banished the rest of her doubts.

When he pulled her blouse out from the waistband of her jeans, she welcomed the touch of his hand on her bare skin. She wanted to get closer, and she returned the favor by pulling his own shirt free and letting her hands travel up the front of his chest.

Reed put his arms around her waist and pulled her over so that he was now lying on his back and she was sprawled across his chest, her hair trailing across the shadow of beard on his chin.

She stared at him, the intensity of his gaze making her feel nervous and worried. She hadn't kissed anyone in a long time. Maybe she had done something wrong. Theo had certainly needed a lot of other women. The thought made her back stiffen as she prepared for rejection, and she pushed herself upright.

The look in Reed's eyes changed to concern. "What's wrong?" he asked.

"I think we're getting a little carried away," she replied, wishing she didn't sound so breathless, so emotionally charged. She pushed herself off him and looked out at the ocean, hoping he would take the hint. He didn't.

"Something happened. You were looking happy and then your eyes changed."

"I guess I just remembered where I was. I'm not the type to make love on a grassy bluff where anyone could walk by."

"Maybe you should try it sometime."

She sent him a quick look. "Have you done this before?"

Reed started to laugh at the jealous edge in her voice. "No, not once. In fact, I've never brought a woman here before. It's kind of my special place, where I come to think."

She didn't know what to say to that remark. Was he trying to tell her she was special? She wanted to believe that he was as caught up with her as she was with him, but she had been fooled before. She cleared her throat and reached for her wineglass. "We should probably finish eating before it gets dark."

"You were thinking about him, weren't you?"

"No."

"Yes, you were."

"I don't want to talk about it."

"I think you're a beautiful, passionate, lovely woman."

Jessica sucked in a deep breath. "And you know just the right things to say."

"I'm not going to hurt you, Jess."

"How can you be so sure?" she asked.

Reed frowned at the plea in her voice. "I know I don't want to hurt you. It's only been a few days, but I feel like you and I could be very good friends. There are no pretenses between us. I can be me, and you can be you. That's pretty rare. As to the future, I don't know."

"I don't, either, but I have to think about it," Jessica said. "Tonight was really special, wonderful in fact. I've had a great time, and—"

"And this sounds like a goodbye speech." He picked up her plate of half-eaten food and handed it to her. "Don't say anything else. Just eat. I kissed you. I think you kissed me back. But it's over—for now. Let's watch the sunset. We'll have time to talk about the rest later."

"All right." Jessica sat quietly, finishing up her chicken and rice salad as they watched the sun dip over the horizon. When the last ray had disappeared, she wrapped her arms around her body as a shiver ran through her.

"Cold?"

"A little."

"We might as well head back."

"Okay." Jessica got to her feet and then looked at her skates. "I suppose those have to go back on."

"Unless you want to get home at midnight."

She made a face and then sat back down again, pushing her feet into the skates while Reed packed up their things. When he had his own skates on, he helped her back to the main pathway and they skated surprisingly smoothly back to the parking lot.

Their ride home was the same, very quiet and a little tense. Jessica wanted to say something, but she didn't know what to say, so she just looked out the window and wondered what was going to happen next. Would he drop her now that she had pushed him away like a frightened teenager or would he still want to see her? And if he did, what would she say?

"Do you mind if I come in?" Reed asked when they pulled into the driveway. "I promised Andrew I'd play one of the games with him, and then I'll take Brandi home."

"Of course."

"Good."

The first thing Jessica heard when she walked in the house was the sound of Andrew laughing. She followed it all the way into the kitchen where two heads were bent close together over a messy pile of Play Doh.

"Hi, honey," she said, finally breaking their concentration.

Andrew looked up with an expression of pride. "Look what I made."

Jessica looked and looked at the purple, pink and green glob in her son's hands and couldn't for the life of her figure out what it was. "Good job."

Andrew made a face. "Don't you know what it is?"

"Well, um . . ."

"Everybody knows that's a dog," Reed said easily. "Looks like old Poppy, as a matter of fact. I like the pink spots, Brandi, nice touch."

Brandi giggled. "We didn't have any black and white clay."

Reed put a hand on Andrew's shoulder. "Can I tear you away, buddy, for a quick game? You did promise to show me your computer."

"All right." Andrew leaped from his chair and Reed swung him into his arms as they left the kitchen.

"I'll clean this up," Brandi said quickly. "I didn't think you'd be back so soon."

"I can take care of it, Brandi. I appreciate your watching Andrew."

"No problem. He's a great kid and easy, too. He actually wanted to do his homework."

Jessica smiled. "It's amazing, isn't it?"

"How did you like roller-blading?"

"It was definitely an experience. You're probably pretty good at it."

"Yeah. Uncle Reed and I go out sometimes on the weekends. He bought the skates you used for my mom when she started going to AA. He thought it would give her something to do when she got stressed out."

Brandi spoke in such a matter-of-fact tone that it took Jessica a moment to realize what she was saying, and then she decided she had better tread carefully. "Did it work?"

"Sort of. I think she'd rather lie on the beach than skate by it." Brandi scooped up the last bit of Play Doh and placed it back in the container. "I'm just glad she's stopped drinking. It was getting pretty scary."

"I'm sure that must have been hard on you."

"Uncle Reed helped out. He told me I could call him if I ever got scared. He's really cool. He always tells me the truth. He says he doesn't want me to make the same mistakes he and my mom made." Brandi sat down on the chair and gave Jessica a quizzical look. "Are you and my uncle—you know—going out?"

Jessica stared at her and then busied herself with finding a sponge to wipe off the table. "We're friends," she said finally, hoping the questions weren't going to get any deeper.

"Uncle Reed says he's never going to get married."

"That's up to him, isn't it?"

"I think he's crazy. I want to get married. I want to walk down the aisle in a long white dress with a train and a veil. I think veils make you look really hot."

Jessica smiled. "I think you have plenty of time to plan your wedding. You're only fourteen."

"My mom had me when she was fiftcen," Brandi said. "But I'm not going to get pregnant till I'm really old, at least twenty-three."

"That's good," Jessica muttered, her mind still grappling with the facts Brandi was so casually dishing out. No wonder Reed had looked so pained when he mentioned his family. It obviously had something to do with his errant sister.

Reed opened the door to the kitchen then, his sharp eyes narrowing when he met her gaze. She felt guilty even though the revelation had all been on Brandi's side.

"You ready to leave, Brandi?" he asked.

"Sure."

Reed handed her the car keys. "I'll meet you outside."

"Okay. Bye, Mrs. Blake."

"Wait, I haven't paid you."

"Uncle Reed took care of it," Brandi explained, waving goodbye as she walked out the door.

Reed's intent gaze made her uncomfortable, and Jessica started wiping down the table again, so she wouldn't have to look at him.

"What did I interrupt, Jess?"

"Nothing. Actually, Brandi was telling me about her mother."

"What about her mother?"

Jessica hesitated, looked up at his stony face and then back down at the table. "She mentioned something about going to AA and getting pregnant at fifteen."

"In other words, Brandi spilled her guts."

Jessica sighed and stopped her scrubbing. "I'm sorry, Reed. I really didn't encourage it."

"Forget it. I can't fault her for telling the truth, and I sure as hell don't want her to keep it to herself if it makes her feel better to shout it to the world."

Jessica studied the tension in his face and wished she could say something to soften the tight line drawing his lips together. "Do you want to talk about it?"

"No."

His answer was abrupt, and Jessica couldn't help but feel a little hurt. "Fine." She walked over to the sink and ran some cool water against the sponge, twisting it again and again as the dirty water ran down the drain.

"Hayley was my responsibility," Reed said.

Jessica turned off the faucet and faced him, waiting for him to continue.

"I was the one who was supposed to watch over her, make sure she was okay, while my mother was working. But I messed things up. Hayley started drinking, ran with the wrong crowd and got pregnant. After that, she tried to commit suicide. Almost did it, too. I found her lying on the bathroom floor in a puddle of blood. As you can see, I did a fantastic job."

"But you couldn't have been much older than Hayley."

"Three and a half years. It was enough. I don't have any excuses. I'm just not cut out to watch over anyone. Hayley finally got professional help, and is hopefully going to be okay, but it's taken her a long time."

"And that's why you're never going to have children or even a wife," Jessica said, feeling a wrench of pain in her stomach as she said the words.

"Right. I would only hurt them in the long run."

"How can you be so sure? You're a grown man now, not a teenager who was trying to take on more than he could handle."

Reed shook his head, obviously dismissing her comments. "I better go."

"You rescued that girl the other day. You saved her life."

"No, Bill did. I saw her lying on the floor and something inside me snapped. She looked just like Hayley. I couldn't move. I'm not a hero, Jess, not by a long shot. Don't make me out to be one."

"You're being pretty hard on yourself, and I can understand that. When my marriage broke up, I blamed myself. I thought I could have done things differently, but sometimes you have to realize that circumstances, not just people, are to blame. Your father was the one who ran off and left Hayley, not you."

He ran a hand through his hair in frustration. "I know that, but it doesn't change things. Maybe I didn't leave town, but I wasn't around for Hayley to talk to. I was too caught up in my own life, and she paid the price."

"And you don't think you've changed any in the past fifteen years? Come on, Reed, that was a long time ago."

"Not long enough for me to forget." He shrugged his shoulders. "I better go. Brandi is waiting."

"You're watching over Brandi," Jessica said, halting him as he turned to leave. "And she loves you."

Reed paused with his back still to her. "Brandi loves her mother, I'm just her uncle, and in the end she is

Hayley's responsibility. I just offer a little moral support now and then.''

"Is that really all?"

Reed went through the door without answering and Jessica sank down into the kitchen chair, emotionally drained by the evening. She closed her eyes and tried to make sense of everything she had learned, but the facts didn't add up. He said he didn't want commitment or responsibility, but he didn't turn his back on people. Maybe he had hesitated for a second during the fire, but she knew instinctively that when it came right down to it, he still would have saved that girl.

She sighed. Maybe he was right, and she just wanted to believe he was better than he was. So where did that leave her? Nowhere. Picking up the sponge, she began to wipe down the counter as Andrew walked back into the kitchen.

"Can I go roller-blading some time?" Andrew asked.

Jessica smiled as she patted down the cowlick that perpetually attacked the back of his head. "Sure. It was fun."

"Maybe Reed will take us."

"Even if he doesn't, we can go on our own."

"But, Mom—" Andrew's words were cut off by the ringing of the doorbell, and they looked at each other in surprise.

"Maybe Reed came back after taking Brandi home," Andrew said with excitement as he raced to the front door.

Jessica followed a little more slowly, not sure if she had the strength to go another round with him tonight. Andrew was about to fling open the door when

Jessica cautioned him. "Remember to ask who it is first."

"Who is it?"

There was no reply, and Jessica frowned, walking over to the door and peering out of the peephole. She couldn't see anyone. After a momentary hesitation, she turned back the lock on the door and opened it slightly.

"Señora Blake."

The childish voice brought her gaze down to Rosa Guerrero and her sister, Juanita. Rosa had her arm around Juanita's thin little body, and two pairs of big black eyes looked up at her.

"Juanita. Rosa. What's wrong?" Jessica asked, pulling the door open so they could enter. "Come in. Tell me what happened. I've been so worried about you."

Juanita was sniffling as they entered, teardrops beginning to trail down her face as they stood inside the entryway. Rosa put an arm around her sister and faced Jessica bravely.

"Papa, no come home."

"Your father didn't come home?" Jessica repeated blankly. "Is he at work?"

Rosa shook her head. "I called the number he gave me. No one answered."

At her sister's response, little Juanita began to cry in earnest and Jessica instinctively gathered her into her arms.

"It's okay, honey. We'll get this sorted out." Jessica smiled down at Rosa's worried face. "Let's go in the living room, and you can tell me everything that you know. I've been trying to call your father for the last two days. Why weren't you in school today?"

Jessica sat down in a chair, pulling Juanita onto her lap as Rosa sat down on the couch with Andrew watching them expectantly.

Rosa took a deep breath. "We were afraid to go to school."

"Why?"

"Because Papa doesn't come home."

"You said that before. Now, when did your father say he was going to be home?"

Rosa shook her head, her eyes starting to fill with tears as she bravely tried to stifle them. "I don't remember."

"Okay. That's all right. What about your mother?"

"Mama died."

"Oh, honey, I'm sorry." Jessica paused, giving herself a chance to think. "Do you know where your father works?"

"With the horses."

Jessica looked at her blankly. "The horses?"

"Where they run fast," Rosa added.

"A racetrack?"

"*Sí*. Yes."

"Okay, he works at the racetrack, but he's late tonight. Did he say anything to you before he left this morning? Who was supposed to watch you after school?"

Rosa stared at her and and then shook her head. "He didn't leave this morning. He left three days ago."

"What? But who's been watching you?"

"Me. I take care of Juanita."

Jessica looked at her in disbelief. "But you're only eleven, Rosa. Surely, your father wouldn't leave you alone for that long."

"You have to find him for us."

"Maybe we should call the police."

"No." Rosa's response was filled with terror. "No police. Papa say no police. Never."

Jessica's misgivings increased at this piece of information. Was Mr. Guerrero in some sort of trouble with the law? It was certainly criminal to leave two small girls alone without anyone to take care of them, and the address he had listed at the school was obviously false. But perhaps something had happened to him. An accident maybe, some reason why he couldn't send someone to take care of the girls.

"What are you going to do, Mom?" Andrew asked. "Are you going to call the police?"

"Not just yet," Jessica said quickly as Rosa started to cry. "First off, I think we need some food. Did you eat dinner tonight, honey?"

Rosa shook her head, wiping her eyes with the back of her hand. "No more food. I look in the garbage can, but I only find bad lettuce, and Juanita wouldn't eat it."

Bad lettuce? Jessica was horrified to think that the children had been reduced to going through garbage cans, but she forced herself not to say anything. There would be time enough for explanations.

"Then I'm going to heat up some spaghetti for you." She gently disengaged Juanita's arms from around her neck. "You stay with Rosa and Andrew, and I'm going to get you some food." She handed the television remote control to Andrew. "Why don't you turn the television on, honey? Find something you and the girls can watch."

"Really?" Andrew's eyes lit up at the unexpected treat.

"Yes, but don't get too settled in. As soon as I get the girls something to eat, you're going to bed."

"Are they going to sleep here, too?"

Jessica shrugged her shoulders. "We'll see. Food first."

Walking into the kitchen, she reached into the refrigerator, pulled out the bowl of spaghetti and reheated it, while her mind whirled with dozens of unanswered questions. She had to find out where the children lived. Maybe a neighbor would know where Mr. Guerrero worked and if something had happened to him.

Fixing up two plates of spaghetti, she walked back into the living room. While the girls were eating, she leafed through the phone directory, hoping to find the number for a nearby racetrack.

She finally came upon Del Mar Race Track, and it wasn't too far from their neighborhood. It had to be the place. She dialed the number and waited, hoping for a miracle. Unfortunately, all she got was an answering machine, listing information about events held on the grounds and it didn't sound like anything had to do with horse racing. Another dead end. She hung up the phone.

"Rosa, do you have the phone number your father gave you?"

Rosa dug out a piece of paper and handed it to her. There were no words, just a seven-digit number. Jessica tried the phone again. No answer, and no recording machine to give any indication to the location. She turned to Rosa "How about your address? Do you know it?"

"125 Paloma, number eight."

Jessica nodded. "Good. When you're done eating, I'm going to take you home. Maybe your father will be back, or at least one of the neighbors will know where he is."

"No." Rosa said the word firmly. "Bad men are there."

Jessica looked at her uncertainly. "What do you mean, bad men?"

"They wait for Papa."

"What are you going to do, Mom?" Andrew asked again, irritating her, because she didn't have a clue what she was going to do. It was one thing to take the girls back to their house, but now with bad men waiting there, she would have to reconsider. A woman alone with three children was probably asking for trouble. If only she had someone she could ask to go with her. Reed.

She didn't want to ask for his help. But still, she was desperate. Maybe he knew another number for the racetrack or where Paloma Street was and what kind of neighborhood she would be going into.

"Why don't you call, Reed?" Andrew suggested.

She sent him a frustrated look that he didn't begin to understand, and then she picked up the phone book. After checking the number she dialed the phone and walked out into the hall for privacy. It rang three times before a masculine voice growled a hello in her ear.

"Reed?"

"What's wrong?" he asked immediately.

"Why do you think something's wrong?"

"We didn't exactly part on good terms."

"That wasn't my fault. You were the one who didn't want to talk."

"You're right." He sighed. "I know I reacted too strongly, Jess. I just have a hard time talking about the past. It wasn't a good time for me."

"Maybe you should talk about it. If you want to have a friendship, you have to be willing to share more than just a picnic." Jessica sent a quick look over at the children who had stopped crying and were watching something on the television. "I want to pursue this with you, Reed, but at the moment I have another problem."

"What's up?"

"One of the kids in my class is here with her sister. They don't speak very good English. Their father is apparently missing, and they don't have anywhere to go. I need to know if there is any way to get through to someone at the racetrack, and then—"

"Racetrack? Whoa, Jess. Slow down. What are you talking about?"

"Their father worked with the horses there. Maybe someone knows where he is."

"And maybe you don't want to know."

"What does that mean?"

"Look, why don't you call the police?"

Jessica hesitated. "Because the girls are frightened, and their father told them not to go to the police."

"Even more reason why you should do just that."

"I'm considering it."

"They're not your responsibility, Jess."

"I'm Juanita's teacher, and they're all alone. Do you want me to turn my back on them?" Jessica didn't wait for him to answer before continuing. "Look, forget I called. I'll handle this myself. I'll just take the girls home. If you can't tell me where Paloma is, I'll look on the map."

"Paloma Street?" Reed swore into the phone. "You can't go into that neighborhood alone, especially at night."

"All right. I'll wait till morning and then see what I can find out."

"I'll go with you. What time?"

"You don't have to bother, Reed. I know how you hate to get involved."

"Just tell me what time."

Jessica hesitated. "Seven-thirty, before school starts."

"I'll meet you at your house. In the meantime I'll look into the racetrack connection. Del Mar isn't in season, so there's nothing happening there, but there are a few other training tracks around here. What's the father's name?"

"Carlos Guerrero."

"Okay. I'll check it out."

"Thanks, Reed."

"Don't thank me. You're the one who has to take care of those kids tonight."

Jessica smiled as she looked over at Juanita and saw her fast asleep on the couch. "They'll be fine. But you really don't have to get involved in this if you don't want to. It's not your problem. I wouldn't have called except I didn't know what else to do. Now that I'm calmer, I can probably handle this on my own."

"Tough, independent Jess, huh?"

"I'm trying to be."

"Don't try so hard. Like you said before, sometimes it feels good to be needed." His voice dropped down a notch and Jessica's throat tightened at the tenderness in his words.

"I have to go and take care of the kids."

"All right. I'll meet you tomorrow morning. Try not to worry, Jess. If we put our heads together, I think we can solve this problem and maybe a few other things."

"Good night, Reed." She hung up the phone and walked over to the children.

"Is Reed coming over?" Andrew asked.

"Not tonight." She smiled brightly to reassure them. "Rosa and Juanita can sleep in the guest room tonight, and in the morning, you and I and Reed will go over to their house and see what we can find out." Rosa looked worried at this piece of information and Jessica immediately reassured her. "Don't worry. We're not going to leave you there. But perhaps your father will be home by then."

The optimistic thought followed them all upstairs, but as Jessica got the girls ready for bed, she had a feeling that the worst was still to come.

Chapter Nine

Paloma Street sounded a lot better than it looked, Jessica decided as they traveled down the street in Reed's Jeep. Everywhere she looked there were signs of poverty, and it certainly wasn't the kind of place she would have wanted to raise a child.

"Which one?" Reed asked.

Rosa pointed to a blue apartment building at the far end of the street. There was no one standing on the front stoop or even in the vicinity, but Jessica felt a stirring of uneasiness in the pit of her stomach when Reed pulled up in front.

Reed parked the car and gave her a stern look. "Lock the doors when I get out and stay in the car."

"I think I should be the one to talk to Rosa's father," Jessica protested.

"If he's there, I'll come and get you. Otherwise, stay put."

Jessica nodded, watching with apprehension as Reed pulled open the front door and slipped inside. Even though she wanted to keep the kids lighthearted and unworried, she couldn't think of a single distracting thing to say, so the four of them sat in a tense sort of quiet, watching and waiting.

Reed returned in a little over five minutes, with his hands full of clothes. Jessica flipped the locks on the car, and he slid into the driver's seat.

"The apartment's empty. I grabbed these for the kids."

"Did you try the neighbor's?"

"I knocked on every door on the floor. One woman answered and shut the door in my face. Another one talked to me long enough to tell me that she didn't see, hear or know anything."

"Great. Doesn't anyone care about these kids?" Jessica demanded in frustration.

"You do," Reed replied. "What next?"

"School, I guess. Did your friend find out anything about the racetracks?"

"There's a big training track about five miles north of here and another about fifteen miles up the coast. There are probably hundreds of immigrants working at both of those places. If he's in the country illegally, he may not want to be found."

"I find it hard to believe that he would turn his back on his children."

"I don't," Reed said flatly. "It happens all the time."

Jessica stared at him for a long moment. "Maybe that's true. But I have to keep thinking positively." She turned around in her seat. "Rosa, do you have any idea of the name of the man your father worked for?"

Rosa shook her head. "I don't know." Her eyes started to well up, and her sister took one look at her and burst out crying.

Jessica sighed. "It's okay. We're going to find him, don't worry."

"Maybe you shouldn't make promises you can't keep," Reed said.

"I intend to keep it."

"If you can. You don't know what happened to their father." He flung a quick look over his shoulder and then dropped his voice down to a whisper. "He could be dead."

"Don't say that. Don't even think it."

"I think that you should take these kids to the police."

"I will, but not yet. I can't. They're so little and afraid, and they're counting on me. I think I'm the only one they trust. I want to at least try to find their father before they get thrown into some foster home."

Reed stared straight ahead, his expression grim. "Maybe they would be better off with a family that could speak their language."

"They need more than Spanish, they need compassion and caring. I have to do this."

"Fine. I'll take you to school."

"Thank you. And I do appreciate your coming with us this morning."

"Forget it. Look, I have to go to work this afternoon, so if you need me, try me at the station. I'll be on duty till tomorrow night." He paused. "You know what's going to happen...you're going to get attached to those kids and it'll hurt like hell when they have to leave."

"Maybe I'll take your advice and worry about that tomorrow."

He sent her a wry smile. "Now you want to take my advice. Great."

"I know you're right, Reed, about the police and all. It's just hard to let them go without trying to help."

"There are some things and people you just can't help, Jess. I learned that a long time ago."

"I have to try. I used to believe that I couldn't change anything about my life, but that wasn't true. We do have some control. We just have to learn how to use it."

Reed turned the key into the ignition and pulled the car away from the curb.

By the time school was out that Thursday, Jessica was no closer to a solution than she had been earlier in the morning. Her calls to the training tracks turned up little information. The track offices had lists of workers, but Carlos Guerrero was not on any list, and most of the trainers would be back that weekend, so even if she wanted to talk to them personally she was going to have to wait.

On the way home from school, she went back to Paloma Street, disregarding Reed's suggestion to stay away. She knocked on doors and tried to get information from some of the neighbors, but the most anyone would say was that the man hadn't been seen for several days.

Frustrated by the lack of concern, she took the children back to her house. She knew she was running out of time. She was going to have to go to the police, which was probably what she should have done in the first place. But she couldn't help worrying about what would happen to the girls if she did. They were alone and afraid, and they trusted her. She didn't want to let them down.

Andrew seemed to feel the same way. He had blossomed, taking them under his wing like a mother hen. She couldn't help thinking how far he had come since the days when he barely spoke to anyone and remained glued to his computer monitor. She had made the right decision for Andrew. Now she had to do the right thing for the girls.

On Friday afternoon she called up a social worker from the Department of Social Services that she had met earlier through a school seminar. She wanted to put in a request to keep the children before she went to the police, who would no doubt be bound to take them away and place them in a shelter. The social worker asked her to bring the girls down to the office so she could talk to them as well.

After much discussion and a review of Jessica's background check through the school, it was agreed that the girls could stay with her at least through the weekend, but she would have to bring them back on Monday to talk to a supervisor about long-term care. The social worker also alerted the police and filed a missing persons report on the girls' father.

That night Jessica called up Brandi to watch the children so she could go to her Spanish class. She wanted to talk to Reed about the kids, but more important she just wanted to see him again.

When she slid into her chair, the one next to hers was empty, and as each student came in, her disappointment deepened. He wasn't going to show

The teacher started the class and they went through their preliminary exercises. Fifteen minutes into the class, Reed slipped in the back door with an apologetic look at the teacher and a tender smile in her direction. Flustered, she lost complete track of what the teacher was saying, and it took her a few minutes to catch up again. She was thankful when the class ended. She was going to need better concentration to learn another language, and she certainly didn't have it tonight.

This time, she didn't rush out of class, but waited for Reed. They walked companionably down the hall and outside without either one saying a word. By the time they reached the main campus square, the rest of their classmates had disappeared, and they were alone.

Reed motioned to a bench and she sat down, feeling inexplicably nervous.

"I didn't think you were coming," she said, folding her hands in her lap.

"I had to work an extra half shift. One of the guys got delayed." Reed stretched his legs out in front of him. "I've been thinking about you. I thought I might have gotten a phone call."

"I didn't want to bother you at work."

"You bother me all the time, Jess."

She looked into his deep blue eyes and hastily looked away. "I talked to a social worker today, and I can keep the girls over the weekend while the police look for their father."

"Good. That sounds like a smart move."

"I know. I wasn't getting too far on my own, but I do want to do some checking tomorrow maybe at some of the racetracks up north

"Okay, I'll go with you." He swung his leg over the bench, straddling it, so he was facing her profile. "Did I tell you that I went to school here?"

She looked at him in surprise. "No. Did you major in fire science or something like that?"

He laughed. "No, I majored in surfing and girls. My minor was business. None of the three actually worked out. But I used to walk through this quad after a night class and see kids holding hands or studying together, and I used to wish it was me."

"And it wasn't you? I have a hard time believing you couldn't get a date."

"Oh I got dates, but they all wanted to go out with the wild party guy, so I went along with it to keep up the image."

His eyes connected with hers, and she saw a rueful self-mockery that was very appealing. "I know what you mean. I always knew what I was supposed to be, and I tried to be it." She looked around her, enjoying the warm night air and the sound of the crickets. "It's funny to be sitting here now I feel like I've been on college campuses all my life but never with someone like you, a surfer, a fireman, a wild guy." She smiled with delight. "Since we're sharing fantasies, I'll tell you one of mine."

Reed raised an eyebrow. "Is it X-rated?"

"Of course not. I used to have this dream that I was walking down the hallway of some very old, ivy-covered building, and the classroom doors were all open. You could hear the teachers murmuring as you passed, and you knew that if you did anything, even sneezed, every eye would turn in your direction. So, I pause and I look around." Jessica stopped talking, giving him a mischievous look. "Then I let out this bloodcurdling yell and run through the halls."

Reed grinned. "Are you naked while you're doing this?"

"No, of course not."

"Then it doesn't sound so bad."

"It does to me. I was brought up to always act the right way. It can be very tiring."

Reed stared at her for a long moment. "Let's do it."

She looked at him warily, not liking the gleam in his eyes. "Do what?"

"Run through the hall and scream."

"I couldn't."

"Yes, you could. In fact, I think you need to do it. You'll never be free as long as you're trying to be that perfect woman."

"And I'll probably get kicked out of class if I'm not. I'm a teacher, Reed. I can't disturb other people's classes."

He shook his head. "Not tonight. You're not a teacher or someone's wife or someone's daughter. You're a woman, wild and crazy. Let it loose, Jess. Get rid of all those frustrations."

"I can't. I'm too scared," she whispered, feeling a sense of excitement building within her.

Reed got to his feet and held out a hand. "We'll do it right here, in the quad, the way the kids do after they take their last final. It won't be quite the same, but I think it will still feel good."

Jessica took his hand somewhat reluctantly, looking around at the opened windows in the classroom. "There's no way."

"Most of the classes are already out. I'll go first."
Reed let out a yell that made her jump back in amazement.

"I can't believe you did that."

"Now it's your turn. Come on, Jess," he urged.

She looked at him and felt the tension burst within her. She wanted to be as free as he was. The scream came out of her throat before she could stop it.

Reed laughed and yelled, "We're free. We're free."

Jessica joined in, taking his hand as he started to jog out of the quad. She ran along beside him feeling foolish and crazy and a little bit light-headed. They didn't stop until they reached the parking structure, and Jessica was breathless when they arrived. She leaned back against a pillar and tried to catch her breath.

Reed recovered first, taking her in his arms with a purposefulness that did little to restore her equilibrium. "You look fantastic. I never thought I'd see you like this."

"I never thought I'd look like this. You're a bad influence on me." She tried to brush the hair out of her eyes, but he stilled her hand.

"Don't change a thing. You're perfect."

"Hardly perfect."

"Then you come pretty damn close." His smile faded into seriousness. "I love the way you let loose back there, and I love the way you took those girls into your home without even a second thought. You're a very giving person. I haven't seen much of that in my life, and personally, I've always been a taker."

Jessica shook her head, reaching up a hand to stroke his cheek. "That's not true. You're too hard on yourself. You give to people every day in your job, and you've given me a lot. You've opened my eyes to a whole new world.''

''Then you don't think I'm completely crazy?'' he asked, his good humor returning.

''I didn't say that.''

''Then I might as well keep going.'' He leaned over and kissed her hard on the lips.

Jessica responded like a flower opening up to the sun. He was heat and fire, and she had been cold for too long. She opened her mouth, changing the light mood of the kiss into something deeper, more passionate. When his lips moved away to cover her cheek and jaw, she felt an aching want deep inside of her. It wasn't enough. It wasn't near enough.

Reed finally lifted his head and stared into her eyes. ''If I don't stop, I'm going to carry out another fantasy of mine right here in the parking lot.''

Her lips curved into a smile. ''That sounds intriguing.''

''You don't know the half of it.'' He stepped back and took in a long deep breath and slowly let it out.

Jessica watched him, wondering what he was thinking. ''Why did you stop?'' she asked finally.

He looked at her with a question in his eyes and some other emotion that she couldn't decipher.

''I didn't want to push my luck.''

''Is that the real reason? Or are you starting to feel the same way I am?''

''How are you feeling?''

''Like I'm about to fall over the edge of a cliff.''

''Then we're definitely feeling the same way.''

''I guess that's a start.''

He nodded. ''Yeah, a start. But I can't make any predictions or any promises, not unless I know

"Unless you know you can keep them," Jessica finished, putting a finger over his lips. "I'm not asking for anything. It's enough right now just to be together."

Reed gathered her in his arms and gave her a big hug, his face buried in the curls at the corner of her neck. "Oh, Jess, I have a feeling we're both going to want more before too long."

Saturday dawned and Jessica awoke in good spirits. Everything seemed to be falling into place. She and Reed had reached a level of understanding, and she had two days to locate the missing Carlos Guerrero.

Reed arrived on her doorstep just before nine, bearing donuts, coffee and a loving smile.

"Hi," she said, remembering their passionate embrace the night before. She was tempted to throw herself in his arms, but her common sense and innate caution had resurfaced with the cold light of day. So she simply opened the door and motioned for him to come in.

"How are the kids?" Reed asked, following her into the kitchen.

"They're still a little upset, but getting along okay."

Reed turned as the kitchen door burst open and a seven-year-old whirlwind blew into the room.

"Hi, Reed," Andrew said, stopping a few feet away.

Jessica smiled at her son's eager expression. He looked like he wanted to throw himself into Reed's arms, too, but he was still afraid of his reception. Funny, she felt a little the same way.

Reed gave Andrew a bear hug. "How's it going?"

"Okay. You want to play some games?"

"Maybe later. Right now I need to talk to your mom. I did bring you some donuts, though." He opened the bag as Andrew slid into his chair. "Where are the girls?"

"Taking a bath." Jessica paused as Wiley started barking at the back door. "You better let him out, Andrew. And go with him. I don't want him digging up my flower bed like he did yesterday. You can take your donut with you."

"Okay." Andrew walked cheerfully out the back door, letting it bang behind him.

"He's getting noisier. I like that." Reed took a sip of his coffee. "So, what's on schedule for today?"

"I want to go to those training tracks you mentioned."

"All right, but not with the kids."

"Why not?"

"In case there's a problem or we find out something you don't want them to know."

"We? You're getting involved, Reed."

"I know, and it scares the hell out of me. But if we find the girls' father, that will be one less problem in our lives. Do you want me to call Brandi to baby-sit?"

"No, I'll ask Mrs. Smithers down the street. She's an older woman, very responsible, and we may be gone a long time. I just hope it's not a completely wasted trip."

"I can't believe how many men answer to the name of Carlos," Jessica complained as they tramped out of one barn and headed for the next.

"One more stable, and we're done," Reed said.

Jessica nodded, following him down the path. She didn't want to give up, but she had to admit it was beginning to look hopeless.

There was a tall, blond man working with a horse and she approached him forcing on a bright, optimistic smile. "Hello, there."

He looked up, a large scar jagging across his face preventing him from smiling. "What do you want?"

"I'm looking for a man named Carlos Guerrero. I wonder if he works here."

The man stared at her for a long moment. "No." He went back to dishing hay into a pile.

"We have his children," Reed added. "They're very worried about their father. If there's anything you can tell us, we'd appreciate it."

"Don't know nothing."

Reed shrugged and turned to Jessica, silently offering her the next move. She shook her head and started walking back to the car. "I think it's hopeless," she muttered, feeling a wave of disappointment crush her spirit.

"You gave it a good shot."

She turned to him with confusion in her eyes. "Do you think these people are lying?"

"I don't know."

"It's so frustrating. Maybe we should have brought the girls. Seeing those two frightened little children might have spurred someone's memory."

"If they're lying, it's because there's a damn good reason. I don't think the kids matter."

Jessica paused as they got to the car, waiting for Reed to unlock her door. "I hate to go back and tell them we came up empty."

"You did your best, Jess. Now it's time for the police to come up with something."

She slid into her seat, thinking about his comment as he walked around to his side of the car. When he had started the car and pulled out onto the highway, she turned sideways in her seat. "Rosa and Juanita will be terrified if they have to leave me."

"They're not your kids."

"I still care about them and worry."

"I think you worry too much." He smiled over at her. "Let's put this morning behind us. We've done everything we can do for now. Let's pick up the kids and have some fun."

Jessica couldn't help the smile that crossed her face. "Fun. That's all you think about."

His blue eyes twinkled mischievously. "That's not all I think about, believe me."

Jessica ignored his comment, but it was impossible to ignore the goose bumps that covered her arms. "What do you want to do?"

"With you or with the kids?"

"With me and the children," she replied firmly.

"In that case, let's go to the pumpkin patch."

Pumpkins and pumpkins and more pumpkins. Jessica had never seen so many in one place, and the kids seemed to be equally bewildered. They ran from one to the next, picking one up and then discarding it for a bigger and better one.

"What do you think?" Reed asked, sidling up behind her. He placed his arms around her waist so that she was pulled up hard against his chest.

She struggled to get free, but he held on tight. "I think I should pick out a pumpkin."

"There's plenty of time for that. The kids want to ride the train. What do you think?"

Jessica looked across the pumpkin patch to where a miniature train was waiting. "Sure. That looks like fun."

"No adults allowed. Looks like you'll be stuck with me for a few minutes—no chaperons."

Jessica slipped out of his embrace and gave him a smile. "I think I can bear it." Then she turned and called for the kids. "Who wants to ride the train?"

The children cheered excitedly, and Jessica took them over to the train depot while Reed bought tickets. When the kids were loaded in, she stood by Reed waving and saying goodbye. Finally, the train pulled away for its five minute tour through the pumpkin fields.

Reed took her hand and pulled her farther down the rail to a cluster of trees.

"Where are we going?" she asked. "Does the train go this way?"

"No, but you and I do."

He pulled her behind the shadow of a big tree and gathered her in his arms. "If I don't kiss you, I'm going to go crazy."

Her heart leaped at his words, and she rested her hands against the breadth of his chest. "What's stopping you?"

"You," he said quizzically.

She shook her head. "Not me."

"In that case…" He lowered his head and kissed her on the lips, gently, tenderly. Then he paused and looked into her eyes. She saw the desire and responded by putting her hands on either side of his face. She kissed him on the corners of his mouth, teasing his lips, until they opened.

He groaned deep down in his chest, thrusting his tongue into her mouth, running it wickedly along the edge of her teeth, capturing her mouth as he was capturing her soul.

The sound of the train horn barely registered, but after a moment, Reed lifted his head and rested his face against hers. "I wish we could be alone together. There's an ache inside of me that just won't go away."

She closed her eyes, as he trailed his mouth down the side of her cheek. She knew just how he felt. "We better get the kids," she said finally, reluctantly.

"Yes, but we're going to continue this—later."

His promising words made her both excited and wary. It was one thing to get caught up in a moment of passion, another to actually set a time for it. "Reed—"

"Don't say anything. The train has pulled into the station.' He took her hand, and they walked back to the depot to collect the children.

During the next hour while the kids laughingly picked out pumpkins, rode ponies and ate popcorn, Jessica would catch Reed looking at her in a strange, unfathomable way, as if she were a problem that he couldn't quite solve. She knew exactly how he felt.

When she watched him with the kids she saw a warm, loving man who had a genuine rapport with all three children. Even Juanita had condescended to holding his hand. He had a way of talking to them that made them laugh and giggle and forget their problems, and she knew it wasn't an act. No one could fake that kind of friendship.

Driving home later that day with three exhausted children and five pumpkins, it was easy to pretend that they were a normal family returning from a day's outing. Of course, there was nothing normal about their group, but for a few minutes she allowed the fantasy, which gradually grew to exclude the children and focus only on her and Reed, a darkened room and a big bed.

She flushed at the thought. She had never had such intense feelings for a man before, and it was frightening. What she had felt for Theo paled in comparison and although she hesitated to admit, even to herself, that she was falling in love, she knew something was happening to her. Something was happening to all of them.

"Can we carve the pumpkins tonight?" Andrew asked as they pulled into the driveway.

Jessica shook her head. "Halloween is still three weeks away. They'll go bad if we open them now."

"Just one, Mom?"

"If I let you do one, then everyone else will want to."

"But Rosa and Juanita might not be here on Halloween."

"He's got a point," Reed said quietly. "What's the harm in cutting the pumpkins? If they go bad, you can always get more."

"I suppose you're right. But I'll only agree if you promise to stay and help."

"Of course. I'm an expert at pumpkin carving."

"That figures."

He flung her a quick grin and then pulled the Jeep into her driveway. "Everybody out."

Chapter Ten

"I believe my job is done," Reed declared, standing back to view the line of odd-looking pumpkin faces. The kids started to giggle, and he wagged a reproving finger at them. "No laughing. These pumpkins are serious works of art."

Rosa and Juanita barely understood what he was saying, but they followed Andrew's lead and kept on laughing.

"That one looks like Swamp Man," Andrew declared.

"Really? I thought it looked like your mother."

Jessica flung a kitchen towel at his head. "Watch it, McAllister. And don't get any ideas about hightailing it out of here. We have a big mess to clean up, and I am not doing it alone."

"But I'm an artist. I create. I let others handle the mundane details."

She handed him a sponge. "Start wiping down the table, please."

He made a face. "Do I have to?"

Andrew laughed. "Hey, you sound like me."

"He does, doesn't he?" Jessica replied. "I think it's time for the three of you to get ready for bed. Andrew, please take the girls upstairs, put on your pajamas and brush your teeth. I'll be up as soon as I get rid of this mess."

The children shuffled out of the room and Reed nodded approvingly. "Good idea, Jess. Send the children to bed, so you and I can have some time alone together."

"It's bedtime, that's the only reason I sent them upstairs," she said, eyeing him warily. "Maybe you should go home. It's been a long day."

"It has been long and frustrating." He set his towel down on the table and walked toward her.

Jessica instinctively backed up toward the counter. "What are you doing?"

"Nothing."

"When Andrew says that, it usually means disaster."

Reed's lips quirked into an irresistible curve. "This won't be a disaster, I promise you."

He stopped a few inches away from her and just looked at her for a long moment.

Jessica had to fight off a temptation to reach up and touch his face with her hand, to kiss him again, to take him upstairs and lock the door. She swallowed hard at the unwelcome thoughts. She had responsibilities to think of, children waiting for her attention.

"I should make sure the kids are brushing their teeth," she said.

Reed planted a hand on either side of her waist, trapping her in the circle of his arms. "They're fine. And I'm sure they'll be down to interrupt us soon enough."

"You don't sound like you mind."

"I do mind, but I realize this isn't the best time or place. Sometimes you have to make do with what you have."

Jessica licked her lips in a nervous gesture. "Are you going to kiss me or what?"

Reed started to laugh. "Getting impatient, huh?"

"No, I just—I don't know what to expect with you."

"That's good, because I feel the same way about you." He leaned over and kissed her on the cheek, a chaste gesture that only made her want more. "I can't seem to stop thinking about you. Even when I'm working, I look into the fire, and the flames remind me of your hair." He turned her face with his hand and kissed her on the other cheek. "When I went surfing this morning and looked into the water, I felt like I was staring into your eyes."

"But my eyes are blue, not green."

He smiled as he kissed her forehead. "Hush, I'm on a roll here."

"Just shut up and kiss me."

"If you insist."

The touch of his lips provided brief satisfaction, but it wasn't enough. She wanted to run her fingers down his spine and explore the body that was resting so tantalizingly against hers.

Reed must have been feeling the same way, because he broke away from her mouth to trail kisses along her cheekbone and down her neck. Jessica closed her eyes, reveling in the delicious sensation, until the kitchen door swung open and she heard a shocked, "Mom!"

Jessica broke away to look into Andrew's startled face. "What's wrong, honey?"

"You were kissing him."

"Actually, I was kissing her," Reed replied.

Andrew looked confused. "Juanita threw up in the bathroom."

"Oh no," Jessica wailed. "Okay, I'm coming."

Jessica jogged up the stairs to find Juanita bent over the toilet bowl with Rosa holding her as best she could. Jessica knelt down and wrapped her arms around her.

"Is she okay?" Reed asked.

"She doesn't feel warm," Jessica replied, placing a hand on Juanita's forehead. "Maybe she ate too much. We did have a lot of popcorn." She grabbed a washcloth off the rail and dampened it in the sink and then tenderly applied it to Juanita's forehead. "Come on, honey, let's get you into bed." As she started to walk out of the bathroom, she looked over at Reed. "You might as well go home. I have my hands full. I'm sorry."

Reed didn't reply as he watched her carry Juanita into the bedroom with Rosa following close behind. He wanted to leave, and he wanted to stay. He felt torn in a way that reminded him of the past, and as much as he hated the feeling, there was something almost comforting about it.

"Are you going to clean that up?" Andrew asked, dragging his attention back to the matter at hand. "Or is Mom going to do it?"

"Your mother is busy. Why don't I tackle it?"

"You?"

"Sure, why not?"

"My dad never cleaned. He said it was woman's work."

Reed grimaced but didn't say anything. "I think when you're a family, everyone has to pitch in and help."

"But you're not in our family."

"So, I'm a friend, that's close enough." Reed took a towel and wiped up the mess from the floor. Then he tossed the towel into the dirty clothes hamper. Turning to Andrew he asked, "Are you ready for bed?"

"I haven't done my teeth yet."

"Then do it."

"Okay."

Reed finished sprucing up the bathroom while Andrew brushed his teeth and washed his face. Then he took him into the bedroom and tucked him into bed.

"Are you going to read me a story?" Andrew asked.

"A story, huh? Does your mom read to you at night?"

"Yes. She likes to do it, but she didn't read to me much when we lived in Boston. My dad used to say that stories were for babies. Do you think I'm a baby?"

Reed sat down on the bed. "No way. You're a big, bad dude."

Andrew beamed with pleasure. "Some of the kids at school say I'm a nerd 'cause I'm smart."

"That's because they're pretty dumb."

"I think so, too." Andrew paused. "But sometimes I don't like it very much."

"No one likes to be called names. You know, when I was in school, the other kids used to think I was tough. I'd go out surfing on the weekends and I was wild. The problem was, I started to believe the things they were saying about me. I thought I was cool, because that's what everyone said."

"But you weren't?"

"No way. I was a marshmallow inside, only I didn't want to admit it. One day, during the middle of a storm, a bunch of the kids dared me to go out and ride a wave. There were all kinds of warnings about riptides, but I just ignored them."

"Did you get hurt?"

"No, but I could have. I tried to take on this wave, and it must have swelled to thirty or forty feet, well maybe twenty. Anyway, my board flew out from under me like someone had yanked it with a rope, and I went flying. I was under the water so long I thought I was going to drown. I kept swimming and swimming, trying to get back to shore, and the ocean kept pushing me back. Finally, I caught a new current, and managed to get to the beach. I was so exhausted, I just laid there and looked up at the sky and thanked God he had saved my stupid hide."

Reed looked down at Andrew. "You have to believe in yourself and how you feel about things. If you listen to other people, you can get into big trouble."

"But you are tough. You ran into that burning building and rescued that girl."

Reed inwardly winced at the reminder. "I did manage to get that girl out, but I also train for that kind of thing every day. I was taking a risk, but I knew what I was up against. Riding a wave in a storm just to impress my friends was stupid, not smart. So the next time they call you nerd, let it blow on by. Be friends with the kids you like and forget about the rest. They don't matter."

"Okay. Good night, Reed."

"Good night, buddy."

"Wait. I forgot to say my prayers."

Reed looked at him in amazement. He hadn't said a prayer in twenty-five years. He didn't think kids did that anymore. But while he was trying to think of what to say, Andrew had scrambled out of bed and knelt down, his hands pressed together in front of him. He murmured a few obligatory sentences and then got on to his personal life.

"God bless Mommy and Daddy, even though he doesn't live with us anymore, and Grandma and Grandpa, even though they got mad when we moved away, and Juanita and Rosa." He paused for a long moment. "And God bless Reed, my best friend."

Reed sucked in a breath at the heartfelt plea and felt a suspicious moisture in his eyes when Andrew looked up at him. "Thanks. I can use the help," he said, as he helped Andrew back into bed. He tucked Andrew in, incredibly touched by the boy's prayer.

"Are you going to marry Mommy?" Andrew asked, startling him once again.

"Why do you ask me that?"

"You were kissing her."

"That's because I like her, but marriage is a big step. It's not something you get into without doing a lot of thinking first, and your mom and I haven't known each other very long." Reed stumbled over the words, wondering if he sounded like a complete idiot.

"I'd like it if you got married. Then we could be a family. And maybe Juanita and Rosa could stay, too."

Reed held up a hand to slow him down. "Whoa, buddy. Juanita and Rosa are in someone else's family. We're going to find their father and get them all back together. You want that to happen, don't you?"

"I like having them here. It's fun. And Mom's happy when you're around."

"She is?" The question tumbled out before he could stop it.

"I heard her tell her friend that you were cute."

Reed smiled wryly. Cute, huh? It wasn't quite what he had in mind, but it was a start.

"You better get some sleep, Andrew." With one last pat of the covers around Andrew's slim body, he switched off the light and walked to the door. He paused there, studying the blond glint of Andrew's hair in the glow from the clown night-light. He felt an incredible sense of belonging that both scared him and beckoned to him.

"Reed," Andrew said softly.

"What?"

"I love you."

It was a whispered confession, and Reed bit down on his lips so hard he could taste blood. Then he shut the door and walked down the hall. He paused on the landing by the stairs. Jessica was singing softly to the girls. It was a lullaby, the words promising sweet dreams and golden mornings. He closed his eyes and listened, wanting to believe, but his emotions were scaring him to death. He was getting too comfortable with Jess and Andrew, beginning to feel a part of their lives. He had to get away before it was too late.

He jogged down the stairs and headed for the front door, but then he remembered the mess in the kitchen. He was running out on her, leaving her to mop up. No, if he was going to end things, he would do it cleanly. He forced himself to walk into the kitchen, hoping she wouldn't come down while he was still there. If he saw her again...if he let himself kiss her again...he might never leave.

Jessica was just coming out of Juanita's room when she heard the front door close. For a split second she was tempted to run after Reed, but the fact that he was leaving only reinforced her doubts. He was fine when things were good, but could she count on him when things got tough?

The unanswered question left a sour taste in her mouth, and she walked into the bathroom to get a drink of water and clean up. To her surprise, the bathroom was in perfect condition with the distant smell of air freshener still lingering in the air.

Then she walked into Andrew's room, prepared to see her son working away at the computer on some game. Instead, she found him fast asleep in his bed. With a smile of tenderness, she leaned over and kissed him on the cheek.

Andrew stirred at the touch and opened one eye sleepily. "Mom?"

"Yes, honey."

"Is Reed coming back tomorrow?" Andrew blinked and then fell back asleep.

"I hope so," Jessica whispered. "I hope so."

Reed stayed away on Sunday, spending the day waxing his car and trying not to think about Jessica or Andrew or the two little girls with the big brown eyes. He had done the unthinkable, he had gotten too close. He didn't want Andrew—or even Jess, for that matter—to love him or depend on him. Free and single had always been his style.

Maybe it was time for a change. The thought came into his mind, and he couldn't suppress it. Jessica and the kids had started him thinking in a whole new direction.

A young voice called out to him, and for an instant he panicked. Then he realized it was his niece, Brandi, not one of Jessica's group.

"I'm in the garage," he shouted, walking around the side of the car.

Brandi and her mother, Hayley, walked in, both wearing dresses. He raised his eyebrows in acknowledgement. "What's the occasion?"

"We just went to church," Brandi announced, looking very proud of herself.

"Church, huh?"

"You look so surprised," Hayley drawled.

His sister had a warm smile on her face that he hadn't seen in a long time, and her blond hair was curled and styled away from her face. Nothing could take the age out of her eyes, but she actually looked young and hopeful. He couldn't remember her ever looking like that. "I am surprised. It's not your usual hangout."

"It might be in the future." She turned to her daughter. "Brandi, do you think I could talk to Reed alone for a minute?"

"Sure, Mom. Can I get something to drink?"

"Help yourself," Reed answered. He watched Hayley through narrowed eyes as she walked over to shut the connecting door between the house and the garage. "Well?"

"I met someone, Reed, someone good."

He groaned. "Not again."

"No, you have the wrong idea. It was at AA. I've been going the last couple of weeks, and I've gotten to be friends with someone. He's a minister, Reed. His name is Marcus, and he's a reformed alcoholic, but what's so great about him is that he really listens to me, and he understands."

"I don't know what to say, except to caution you about getting involved too fast."

Hayley laughed. "That's all you ever do is caution me. I know I've needed it in the past, but I think I'm on the right track now." She took a breath and paused. "I tried to find Dad."

"You did what?" he thundered. "Are you crazy? Didn't he give us enough grief?"

"Marcus suggested it. He said he thought I had a lot of unresolved feelings about Dad, and he was right. I never forgave him for leaving us. That's why I did all those stupid things."

Reed fiddled with the towel in his hand and then looked at Hayley. "Did you find him?"

"Yes, at a bar near a racetrack up north. He looked bad, Reed, old and weary. He was drinking, and when I saw him, I saw me." Hayley's voice tightened. "It was a shocking sight, let me tell you. I don't want Brandi to ever look at me and see that. I'm going to change, Reed. This time I'm really going to do it."

"I hope you can. You know I'm behind you."

Hayley nodded, offering him a wry smile. "I also know you blame yourself for things I did. I guess I used to let you think that way because I wanted someone to care about me, but I know now that I have to help myself. No one else can do it for me."

"Just don't rely on this guy too much, Hayley. Stand on your own feet."

She smiled broadly. "I intend to, and Marcus wouldn't have it any other way. Now, I just wish I could convince you to change a little bit."

"I'm happy the way I am. I've got a great job, a nice house on the beach—"

"And no woman or family. We've both been running from ourselves for a long time, Reed. I've finally stopped. Maybe you should, too."

Reed stared at her for a long moment, hearing what she said, but not willing to let go, not quite yet. He wanted to believe her, but she hadn't always kept her promises. "I'll think about it."

"Good. And I'd like to meet your Jess sometime. Brandi says she's gorgeous."

"Yeah, well, I don't know if that's going to be happening any time soon. She's got a kid, you know."

Hayley nodded in understanding. "I wish you luck."

"Thanks, I'll need it. Where are you off to now?"

"Brunch with my daughter. It's time we did some talking."

"Sometimes you have to do more than just talk, Hayley. Show her how you feel with the way you act."

Hayley walked over to the door. "That's good advice. Maybe you should do the same thing."

Reed made a face as she walked out the door and began polishing his car, but her words kept going around and around in his head. Maybe it was time for a change. Everybody else seemed to be moving along but him. He scrubbed impatiently at a speck of dirt on the car door. It wouldn't come out. It was stubborn and unyielding, reminding him a little of himself.

By late afternoon on Sunday, Jessica's nerves were strung out like a taut wire. She flinched every time the phone rang, hoping it was Reed. He hadn't called or come by. She told herself that she wasn't surprised. Dating her wasn't exactly a walk on the wild side, not with kids and a dog and all kinds of problems following her around. Still, she was disappointed, and the kids were, too.

After one hundred questions about Reed, she had piled them into the car and gone to the movies. Juanita had fallen asleep during the cartoon and Andrew and Rosa had stuffed themselves with popcorn to the point of happy oblivion. It was one way to pass the afternoon.

She was just searching through the cupboards for dinner fixings when the doorbell rang, and despite her best intentions, her heart jumped into her throat. She had to force herself not to run to the front door, but when she opened it, she couldn't repress a beaming smile.

"Reed."

He smiled back. "Hi, Jess." He walked in and gave her a searing kiss on the lips. "I missed you today."

"Really?" she asked hopefully, then mentally scolded herself for being so revealing. "We went to the movies."

"So, you didn't miss me at all?"

She shrugged, holding her fingers an inch apart. "Maybe this much."

"Thanks," he said with a wry smile. "You're great for my ego. Where are the little Munchkins?"

"Playing upstairs. Do you want me to get them?"

"No." He walked toward the living room. "Maybe the two of us can have a moment of privacy."

Jessica followed him into the living room, watching as he sat down on the couch. "What do you want to talk about?"

"Come here," he said softly.

She didn't trust the look in his eyes. "Why?"

"Because you're too far away."

Jessica hesitated and then slowly walked over to the couch. She had every intention of sitting a good distance away from him, but his arm snaked out around her waist and pulled her down on his lap.

"Reed. I can't sit here. The kids might come in." She wiggled in an attempt to scoot off his lap.

"If you keep doing that, we're going to be even more embarrassed."

She flushed at his comment and stopped moving. "Fine. Say what you have to say and then let me go."

"I'm not sure I can let you go," he said half seriously, half joking. "That's the problem. I try to stay away, but my car keeps bringing me back."

"Has a mind of it's own, does it?"

"I'm afraid so." He wrapped his arms around her and squeezed tight. "Are you completely over your ex-husband?"

She looked at him in surprise. "That's a strange question."

"Could you answer it?"

"I've been over Theo for a long time, years before we got the divorce."

"And no regrets?"

"About divorcing him—no. About marrying him—yes. But I already told you that."

"I know, but I guess I just wanted to be sure that you were really free."

She studied him thoughtfully. "Free to do what?"

''Be with someone else. Maybe me.''

''Maybe you? Doesn't sound like you're too sure you want me.''

''Oh, I want you. I'm just not sure it's in either of our best interests. I'm afraid I'm like my dad, that I won't make it for the long haul.''

''You won't know until you try.''

His eyes searched hers for something more. She wanted to tell him what he needed to hear, but she wasn't sure what that was.

''Could you take a chance on someone who might not make it long term?'' he asked.

His question hit her hard. It was something she had been asking herself as well. ''I don't know. But I don't think you give yourself enough credit. You're not your father. You haven't walked out on your family or your friends, not even when things have gotten a little sticky.''

''But I might.''

She smiled at the stubborn set of his jaw. ''And I thought I worried a lot.''

Reed met her gaze and tipped his head in acknowledgment. ''You're right. I'm thinking about the future even though I've always told myself not to do that. But when I'm not worrying about the future, all I can think about is you and your ridiculous buttons.'' He reached out and deliberately unbuttoned the top button of her blouse. ''I'd like to make love to you for about a month straight, and that's just for starters.''

His words stirred up her emotions, and she couldn't think of a clear-cut answer, especially while she was wrapped in his arms like a cherished present.

''I feel the same way,'' she murmured.

He groaned. "Don't tell me that. One of us has got to fight this."

"You've changed me, Reed, the way I think, the way I feel, and it's hard to change back. I still worry about what might happen, how it might affect Andrew, but I also worry about not doing anything, about letting someone like you slip out of my life."

"You might be better off. Sometimes when I see you, I see my mother. She was soft and gentle, and when my dad left, she was completely devastated. It took her years to pick up the pieces and she was never the same after that." He paused. "Now, she's a hard, tough waitress who doesn't take grumbling from anybody. I kind of miss that other woman."

"Everyone changes, Reed. I know I did when I found out about Theo. He took my innocence away." She blinked back a sudden rush of moisture behind her eyes. "But he also made me grow up, take responsibility for myself and my happiness. Whatever happens in the future with someone else is going to be my decision, and I'll go into it with my eyes open."

Reed stared at her for a long moment, a dozen emotions chasing through his clear blue eyes. "But if you get hurt again—"

"I'll deal with it," she finished.

"What are you saying, Jess?"

Her confidence faltered at the question. It was easier to talk in generalities than in specifics. "I don't know. What are you saying?"

He smiled, shaking his head. "Hell, if I know." He hugged her tight. "I don't know why I'm laying all this on you now. I know you've got the girls on your mind, and Andrew "

"That's true. And even if the girls go away, I'll still have Andrew." She pulled back so she could look into his eyes. "I won't make a decision without thinking long and hard about his welfare."

"I don't think you should." He dropped his gaze. "That's part of the problem, Jess. When I tucked him in last night, I realized how attached he was getting, and how I swore I wouldn't hurt either of you."

She put a finger over his lips. "Now this is starting to sound like your goodbye speech, and like you told me before, we don't have to make any decisions right now."

Reed looked at her for a long moment. "All right. We'll put things on hold for a few days. Actually, I did come by to give you something." He reached into his pocket and pulled out a torn white envelope. "I went by the girls' apartment again, just to see if there was something that I missed, and I found this envelope. There's a name, Louisa, and also an address." He handed it to her. "Maybe it's something for the police to go on."

Jessica took the envelope and nodded. "This might be just what we need."

"I'm afraid we need more that that," he said, his expression turning somber.

"I thought you didn't want to talk about us."

"I don't want to talk." His eyes darkened with emotion and he pressed her close against him, burying his face in her hair. "Just let me hold you for a little while."

Jessica put her arms around him in reply, wishing they both weren't so afraid to love.

Chapter Eleven

Monday afternoon, another bright and sunny day in southern California. It would be more appropriate if there were doom and gloom, Jessica thought, as she drove the children downtown to see another social worker about foster care. She had spent an hour after school preparing them for the experience, and despite their protests and solemn faces, she stood firm. She reassured them it would be all right and hoped with all her heart that it would be.

By the end of two hours, the kids were grumpy and unhappy, and Jessica felt exactly the same way. She had answered question after question. She didn't know what they wanted her to say, but she obviously wasn't saying it. She didn't have any answers about the children's father and little information about any other part of their life. She just knew that she wanted to protect them.

When the supervisor suggested putting the children into a foster home, they wailed, not knowing the exact content of her words, only her intention to take them away from Jessica.

"I would like to keep them with me until you find out something," Jessica said firmly.

The social worker tapped her pencil on the desk and gave her a speculative look. "It's not our usual policy, but my colleague, who you met with on Friday, assured me that you were very responsible. We would prefer, however, that you were a relative."

"Apparently they don't have any relatives," Jessica said sharply. "They trust me, and I can take good care of them. Surely that's what important here."

"Of course, we want the best for the children, but you do know this may take some time."

"I'm perfectly happy to keep them as long as it takes."

"That's very generous of you." She paused. "We do have a shortage of suitable foster parents, so I'm willing to see if we can work with you. I can do a house inspection with you this evening, and then we'll let things go until we have more information."

Jessica let out a sigh of relief. "Thank you. I think this is the best thing for the children."

The social worker unbent for a moment to smile. "You seem to care a great deal for them."

"Yes, I do." Jessica stood up. "Let's go home, kids."

A week later they were still waiting for answers and when Saturday morning dawned, Jessica felt like they were in the eye of the storm. As she stared out the window at the children playing football in the backyard, everything seemed too perfect. Reed, the biggest kid of all, was being tackled by the girls while Andrew tried to throw him a pass. The game ended in a fit of giggles. Still, she felt uneasy.

Jessica let the curtain drop back into place. The children were momentarily happy, but she knew they still worried about their father, as did she. Even Reed seemed preoccupied, looking unusually somber when the girls would climb in his lap and clamor for a story. To his credit, he spent as much time as possible with them when he was off duty. Sometimes too much time. She couldn't help feeling a little put out that the only attention she got was a heart-stopping, soul-searching kiss on his way out the door.

"Mom," Andrew said, bursting through the back door. "Where's my baseball bat?"

Jessica grinned, her bad mood fading. "You mean the one you've never used? It's in your closet."

"Great. Reed's going to teach me how to hit."

"If that's all right with you," Reed said, following Andrew into the kitchen. He had Juanita in his arms and Rosa by his side, and they were all smiles.

"It's fine, if you're sure you want to."

"No problem. I—"

His words were cut off by the ringing of the doorbell. To Jess it sounded like a clap of thunder. She had a feeling the storm was about to erupt.

"Who's that?" Reed asked.

"I don't know. I guess I better answer it."

They walked to the front door in silence, the girls' laughter dimming at their serious expression. Jessica opened the door and her heart sank. It was the social worker and another woman who looked a little like the girls.

"Louisa," Rosa shouted, suddenly coming alive. She ran into the woman's arms and gave her a big hug.

Juanita didn't look so sure, and she wrapped her arms tight around Reed's neck.

"This is Louisa Cordova," the social worker explained. "She lives at the address you gave us, but unfortunately she was away until yesterday. She's the children's aunt."

"I see," Jessica said slowly. "Won't you come in?"

She led them into the living room and sat down hard on the couch. Reed sat next to her with Juanita still on his lap and Andrew squeezed in tight on his other side.

The social worker smiled at them reassuringly. "Mrs. Cordova believes that the children's father was deported a couple of weeks ago."

"Deported?" Jessica echoed. "I guess that explains why no one can find him."

"He loves his children," Louisa cut in. "I don't know what happened, but I am sure he is very worried about them."

"Then why didn't he tell someone he had children that needed to go with him?" Reed demanded.

Louisa didn't answer and the social worker simply shrugged. "Sometimes they think they'll be right back over the border. But now that we know the circumstances, we can reunite the family. The girls need to come with me today."

Jessica looked at Juanita, snuggled in Reed's arms and felt a deep twinge of pain, but she knew the social worker was right. The children belonged with their father and their family. "I'll get their things," she said quietly.

The girls had not been with her for long, but they had gotten under her skin and entwined themselves around her heart. She knew she would never forget them or the sense of family they had created. It suddenly struck her that she wanted to have that feeling again, a husband and maybe more children, a warm family unit to share life with.

An hour later, their goodbyes were said among a bevy of tears. Jessica placed her hands on Andrew's shoulders as they watched the car pull away from the house.

"You think they'll be okay?" Reed muttered. "What if their father is no good?"

Jessica sent him a tender smile that made him only look more grumpy. "I think they'll be fine. Rosa and Juanita love their father and from what Louisa said he is a good man. He just wanted to make a better life for his children, only he didn't go about it the right way." She paused. "They really got to you, didn't they?"

"A little. I know what it's like to be young and scared about what's happening to you. But it looks like their story is going to have a happy ending."

"I hope so. It's hard to stop caring, isn't it? Even when you don't have a legal commitment, it doesn't stop your heart from loving or breaking."

Reed sent her a deep searching look and then turned his head, staring out at the now empty street.

"Why do they have to leave?" Andrew asked, interrupting their conversation. "Why can't their father come here?"

"It's a long story, honey, but they're better off with him wherever that is. Family is what's important." She forced a smile on her face. "I have an idea. Let's do something adventurous, have some fun. It's still a beautiful day. The sun is shining. The weather is warm."

"Fun. Is that all you think about?" Reed teased.

She laughed. "I think it will take our minds off things. Maybe a swim in the ocean or a hike?"

Reed scoffed at her suggestion. "Too tame, my dear. I think it's time for us to go surfing."

Her smile faded. "No, I couldn't. Absolutely not."

"Surfing?" Andrew asked. "Can I go out with you?"

"Of course," Reed replied.

"No, absolutely not," Jessica said again.

"Sorry, you're outvoted."

Jessica protested all the way upstairs, while Reed stood over her, forcing her to get her swimsuit and sunblock out of her bedroom. On the way to the beach, she told herself that she might allow him to take Andrew out, but only in the shallow water, and if the waves weren't too big. But she was not going to do anything more than lay on the beach and work on her tan.

"We can stop in at my place and leave your things," Reed said, as he pulled into the garage of a town house set right on the beach.

"This is your home?" Jessica asked, following him up the stairs to a simple but beautiful apartment. The living room was open and airy with floor-to-ceiling windows looking over the ocean. The furniture was comfortable and used, just the way she liked it. There were magazines and newspapers spread out on the table and chairs, and she walked around the room, picking up the knickknacks and photos, wanting to get another look into the man who had turned her world upside down.

"Who's this?" she asked, pointing to a photo of Reed and two women.

"My mom and sister," he said shortly. "I'll just change my clothes."

"Take your time. I'll just look around."

"Go ahead and snoop to your heart's content. I leave my incriminating stuff in my locker at work."

There weren't any other photos of interest, but there were a couple of trophies, and Jessica took a minute to read the inscriptions, first place in speed boat racing, a couple of firsts in surfing, and a second place in skydiving. Good Lord, he really did like to take risks. Maybe she should count her blessings that they were only going surfing and not jumping out of an airplane.

Correction, she was not going surfing. Andrew and Reed were going to balance on a board in knee-deep water so her son could forget about missing the girls. That was it.

But Andrew and Reed had other ideas. Jessica watched in alarm as Reed moved his training lesson from the stable sand to the water.

"I don't think he's old enough to do this," she called out, bringing a look of disgust from her son.

"We're just going to get used to the water," Reed replied. "Don't worry."

Jessica bit back a retort and shaded her eyes with her hand, watching as they went out a little farther in the water. Andrew was standing on the board, while Reed kept an arm around his waist. They were only playing in the shallow water, so she relaxed.

Gradually they began to move farther out, and Reed had Andrew lie down on the board and let the wave bring him into the beach. Andrew slid off a couple of times, and he was laughing and glowing with an excitement that made her heart swell. Reed was so perfect with him, encouraging but firm, a buddy who could talk to him without being patronizing.

She felt an ache grow in her stomach and spread upward, settling around her heart. If only he wanted children and a wife. If only he wasn't so afraid to take a risk on loving them. But was she any better? She had played it safe all her life. Her divorce had been her big step toward independence. Maybe it was time to take another one.

Reed and Andrew ran up the beach toward her and Andrew flopped down on the sand, ignoring her offer of a towel.

"It's your turn, Mom."

"No, that's okay. You were doing great, though."

"Just baby stuff," Andrew complained.

Reed shook a finger at him. "You've got to start with the basics. Besides, I think your swimming skills should be a little stronger before we hit the deeper water."

"Can you teach me?"

Reed hesitated. "Maybe. Right now it's your mom's turn."

Jessica immediately shook her head. "I'm not going out there."

"It's like roller-blading. You'll love it."

"I don't think so."

"Can you swim, Jess?"

"Yes, but that's not the point."

"Surfing is an adventure. The new you will love it."

"The new me wants to keep on living."

Reed reached out and grabbed her hand, pulling her to her feet.

She dug her toes into the sand. "I'm not going. I don't want to leave Andrew alone on the beach."

"I'm not a baby, Mom."

"Don't you trust me?" Reed questioned.

"It's not a matter of trust."

"I'm not going to let anything happen to you."

"I think she's scared," Andrew said, jumping into the conversation. "It's fun, Mom."

She gave him a disgusted look and threw up her hands. "Okay, fine. I'll surf. You want me to take a risk, I'll do it. And then when it's your turn..." She let her words drop off, but her meaning was clear.

Reed shook his head. "You're right. You shouldn't do this for me. Do it for yourself. Surfing is a wild, exhilarating ride, but I don't want to force it on you. It has to be your decision."

Put like that, Jessica knew there was only one choice to be made. "Then I say, yes. You only live once, right?"

"Right."

"Andrew, wait here for me, and don't talk to anyone."

Andrew rolled his eyes. "Would you just go so I can have another turn."

Reed laughed and gave her a gentle shove toward the water. "I think that's our cue."

He walked into the water behind her, and she shivered as the cold hit her legs.

"You'll get used to it," Reed said. "Why don't you sit on the board, straddling it with a leg on either side?"

Jessica turned up her lip but did as she was told, getting the feel of the board as it moved with the waves.

"What do you think?"

"Piece of cake."

He laughed. "Good, then we'll take her out a little bit deeper. You go first."

"Where?"

"Out there."

Her courage waned. "That's awfully far."

"The waves are small today."

"Shouldn't I have tried standing on the board, first, like you did with Andrew?"

"No, because I'm going to hold on to you."

For some reason that didn't entirely reassure her. She wanted to concentrate, and the thought of her nearly bare body against his nearly bare body was very distracting.

He shook his head at her doubtful look. "Okay, if you want to stand on the board a couple of times, we'll do it right here. Go ahead and get up."

Jessica did so and immediately slipped off, landing on her bottom. "Why do I keep falling for you?" she asked crossly.

"Must be my charm. Try it again."

This time she was pleasantly surprised as she managed to stand up with his arm around her waist while the last foot of water carried them back to the dry sand. "Not bad. Okay, I'm done."

"Wrong. Lie down on your stomach on the board."

"Why?"

"Just do it."

When she was lying down, he put his arm across her back and began pushing them out toward the deeper water. It was smooth and fun, and she liked the feel of his hand on her. There was a watery moment when they got through a breaking wave, but other than getting a good drenching, she was still on the board in good condition. Pretty soon they were deep enough that Reed had to start treading water.

"Now scoot up on your knees," he commanded, hauling himself onto the board when she had done so.

She held on for dear life as the board rocked precariously. Finally, he was sitting behind her, one arm wrapped around her waist.

"Now what?" she asked.

He leaned over and kissed her ear, letting his tongue dart into the corners. She gasped. "Are you crazy? You're going to drown both of us."

"But what a way to go."

"Would you be serious? What if a wave comes along while you're doing that?"

He kissed her neck while the fingers of his right hand spread out across her stomach, making her wonder just how far he intended to go. She risked releasing her grip on the board to place her hand firmly on his.

"Andrew is watching," she snapped. "Did you bring me out here to surf or fool around?"

"Do you want to know the truth?"

She turned her head so she could send him a stern look, but the smile in his eyes made the anger quickly fade. She didn't want to scold him, she wanted to kiss him properly without being on a surfboard in the middle of the ocean with her son watching. "You're crazy."

"Thank you."

"It wasn't a compliment." She chuckled. "Since I'm out here, why don't we hail a wave or something?"

"That's catch a wave, and I think we have one coming." He looked over his shoulder and began to paddle with his hands.

Jessica felt a moment of panic. "What do I do?" Reed got into a squatting position and then pulled her up beside him. They were standing for at least ten seconds when the wave broke, and they went tumbling into the white water in complete abandon.

Jessica came up spluttering, to find Reed anxiously calling her name. She waved her hand, and his worried eyes connected with hers. In that split second she saw love and fear, and it was so intense she couldn't do anything more than sit in the water and wait for him to come to her.

"Are you all right?" he demanded. "I should never have tried that with you. If anything had happened ..."

"Nothing happened," she said softly. "I'm fine, and that wave was child's play. We both know that. You would never have put me in danger." He didn't look totally convinced, so she continued. "I'm responsible for myself, Reed. I take chances when I decide to do so."

"I talked you into it."

"No, you tried to talk me out of it."

"Oh, Jess. I don't know what's what anymore. I feel like everything is turned upside down." He ran a hand through his wet hair as he stared at her. Then he leaned over and kissed her hard on the lips, uncaring as to who was watching. It was short but filled with emotion, and it said a lot of things he couldn't say with words.

Then he helped her to her feet, and they walked back to join Andrew who had lost interest in their surfing and was actively engaged in building an awe-inspiring sand castle.

Reed took Andrew out on the board again while Jessica dried off in the warm sunshine. She was glad for the breather. She needed time to figure out what she was doing, but thinking about the future seemed too depressing, so instead she closed her eyes and laid back on her towel.

What a long way she had come from a frigid marriage in a cold eastern town to a hot and exciting relationship on a California beach. She had changed so much in the past few years and especially in the past two weeks, that she barely recognized herself. Andrew was changing every day as well. He was turning into the happy, carefree little boy she had always wanted. Their life was good and getting better. They were learning to live, not just to exist, and she knew she would never be satisfied with less ever again. A splash of water across her bare legs sent her eyes flying open and she looked up at a grinning Andrew.

"Were you sleeping, Mom?"

"No, I was resting. Are you two done?"

"Reed is going out by himself."

Jessica sat up and looked out at the water. She could see Reed's bright orange bathing suit in the distance, but he was paddling farther and farther out. Finally he turned and waited, then began his race with the wave building behind him. It was one of the larger waves she had seen all day, but he handled it with ease, balancing his lean, muscular body on the board as if he were standing on a street corner rather than on a slippery piece of waxed surfboard.

His ride seemed to last forever as he cut a path back and forth through the cutting waves. Finally, he hit the end, but instead of joining them on the beach, he went back out. He continued doing that for almost an hour, and Jessica grew more tense with each passing minute. He seemed to be pushing himself to the point of exhaustion, but every time she waved to him, he ignored her.

While Andrew was busy playing in the sand, she waded out toward where the waves were breaking, waiting for Reed's next run. When he came in, she called out to him.

"Are you done?"

Reed looked at her and sighed. "You want to go home?"

"I'm worried about you." She stared at him over the distance of water that separated them.

"Why? I'm fine."

His features didn't support his exuberant response, and her eyes narrowed. "You don't look fine. You look tired and worried."

He turned and walked toward the beach, leaving her to follow. When they got to the shoreline, he started playing with Andrew and, frustrated at their lack of privacy, she sank back down on her towel and wondered what the heck was going through his mind now.

She was pleased that he was playing with her son, but she wondered if he wasn't hiding behind Andrew so he wouldn't have to talk to her. Finally, the heat of the day began to burn off, and they came back to join her.

"I'm starving, Mom," Andrew announced. "Can we get hamburgers?"

"Sure, whatever you want."

Reed looked at her and then directed his gaze back out at the water. "I'll have to pass. I have a meeting tonight."

"A meeting? I thought you were off till tomorrow."

"This is with a recruiter from one of the New York fire stations."

She waited, an uneasy knot growing in her stomach. She didn't like the look in his eyes, and she wasn't sure she wanted to hear his explanation, but finally she had to ask. "Why are you going to talk to him?"

"I've been offered a job in New York City. I'm supposed to give them my answer tonight."

She bit down on her lip, preventing the gasp from crossing her lips. "What is your answer?"

Chapter Twelve

Reed shook his head, looking as troubled as sne felt. "I don't know, Jess. I still have another hour before I have to say yes or no."

"Then maybe we should leave you to it," she said briskly, getting to her feet. "Andrew, get your things together. We'll grab some hamburgers on the way home and get ready for school tomorrow."

Andrew didn't move. He just stood and looked at Reed. "Are you going away?"

Reed squatted down next to him so they were at eye level. "I might have to, buddy."

"Why? Don't you like us anymore?"

"This doesn't have anything to do with you," Reed replied. He looked up at Jess. "Can you help me out here?"

She shook her head. "No."

Reed sighed and gave Andrew a big hug. "I do like you, Andrew. But I've been thinking about this move for a long time. They have big fires in New York City, a chance for me to become the best fireman I can be. I've also lived here all my life. You and your mom made a change by moving out here. I'm thinking maybe I need to change by moving somewhere else. Do you understand?''

"I don't want you to go," Andrew said, his eyes gathering moisture. He rubbed his fist against the corner of his eye and kicked at the sand with his toe.

Reed slowly got to his feet. "Things will work out for the best, you'll see."

Andrew took off running and Jessica felt like following. Instead, she picked up her things and began to walk back to Reed's town house.

"Don't you have anything to say?" Reed asked, after they had been walking in silence.

She didn't answer him right away, but when they got to his back door, she paused and looked at him. "I think you're running away. The biggest challenge is not in New York City, it's right here. I guess you're not up to it. I'd appreciate it if you could take us home now."

Reed watched in dismay as her shoulders stiffened and her face grew taut. She was turning back into the uptight woman he had first encountered, cold and hostile, and he couldn't do a damn thing about it. He couldn't say what she wanted him to say. The words just wouldn't come out.

During the next two weeks Jessica felt like her heart was breaking. Watching Andrew retreat into his shell, waiting for a phone call that would never come and missing the two little girls that had captured her heart, was more than enough to turn her mood into one of depression. The only bright spot was hearing that the girls had been reunited with their father. At least one thing had worked out right.

She didn't know what Reed had decided to do about New York, because he didn't call. Day after day passed, and there was still no word. She missed him with an intensity that seemed out of proportion with the length of time they had known each other, but it hadn't been the quantity of time, it was the quality.

Time would heal them. She knew that with her head, but her heart took a little more consoling, and Andrew refused to even talk about Reed. It was what she had feared all along, that he would fill their lives, and when he left there would only be emptiness. The risk of getting involved with him now seemed foolish. The end had come anyway, and she hadn't even had the chance to experience all the joy she could have.

She was sitting in her classroom checking papers one Friday afternoon, waiting for Andrew's class to get out at three o'clock, when Donna burst in on her, agitation written across her face.

"What's wrong?" Jessica asked immediately.

"It's Andrew."

Jessica jumped to her feet. "Is he hurt?"

"No, he was in the school yard at recess time, and when Mrs. Williams called for the class to line up and count heads, he wasn't there."

"Oh, my God. Someone took my son?"

"No. Jason Conroy said that Andrew told him he was leaving, that he had to go see someone."

"He had to see someone?" Jessica echoed in a daze. Her mind raced with the possibilities. The only friends he had were at school, and he certainly wouldn't try to get back to Boston on his own. That left only Reed. Of course, Andrew had tried to get her to call him just the night before, but she had refused.

"I have to make some calls." She dashed down the hall to the telephone. She tried Reed's home number first, but there was no answer. Then she called the station, which had the machine running. "I'm going to the fire station," she decided. "If Andrew comes back, call me there."

Donna ripped off a piece of paper and jotted down the number. "We've already alerted the police just in case, and a couple of the aides are searching the school again."

"Thanks, Donna. I just hope he's all right." She bit back a sob that was threatening to spill out. She couldn't afford to be emotional right now. She had to find Andrew first and make things all right.

Bill Carlton shrugged his arms out of his jacket and looked over at Reed. "You look like hell."

Reed rubbed a hand over the scraggly beard on his jaw. "What do you expect? We've been at it for hours."

"And you want to leave here for the excitement of New York?" Bill slammed his locker shut, smiling as Reed winced at the sharp, clanging noise. "Good, now that I've got your attention, I have something to say." He paused. "Are you out of your mind?"

"No. Is that it?"

"Not by a long shot. For a man who's supposed to be thrilled to move to the Big Apple, you've been grumpy for the last two weeks. Are you sure you want to do this?"

"Yes. I'm a rambling man, and it's time to ramble."

Bill snorted in disgust. "Give me a break. You haven't rambled out of this town in years. You never even liked to go away to summer camp when you were a kid."

"Then maybe it's time for me to leave."

"What about the redhead and the cute kid?"

"History. She wants commitment and a father for her son. I'm not cut out for the role."

"How do you know until you try?"

"It's in the genes, Bill. I'm just like my dad, but the difference is, I know my limitations."

"Bull. You've been recycling that excuse for years. You're nothing like your old man. You've got a job. And until now you've never run away from your problems."

"You think that's what I'm doing?"

"Well, isn't it?"

Reed ran a hand through his hair. "I don't know anymore. I can't think straight when I'm around her. Everything seems possible, but when I go home, I remember all the reasons why it won't work. I can't hurt Jessica and Andrew, they've already been through so much."

Bill shrugged his shoulders. "So you're going to leave, start over somewhere else. That should make them real happy. I bet they're jumping for joy right now."

"Just leave me alone."

"Fine. You're free. No one to care about where you're going, just the way you like it."

Reed slammed his locker as the outer door opened. One of the other firemen poked his head in the door.

"McAllister. There's a freckled-face kid out here who looks like he's going to cry."

Reed's jaw dropped. "What?" He sprinted through the station to the kitchen. "Andrew." He held out his arms and Andrew ran into them.

Reed hugged him tightly for a long moment, then held him back so he could see his face. "What are you doing here? Where's your mom?"

"She's at school," Andrew sniffed. "She wouldn't come, so I came by myself."

"By yourself?" Reed felt sick at the thought of Andrew crossing all those busy streets on his own. "Well, at least you're okay. But that was not a smart thing to do."

"I have to talk to you." Andrew looked over his shoulder at the other fireman and hung his head.

Reed turned to Bill, who had followed him into the room. "Call Jessica Blake at Crestmoor Elementary School and let her know Andrew is here. We'll wait for her out front."

Reed led Andrew out the back door and over to the brick wall that ran alongside the firehouse. He propped Andrew up on the wall so they could look each other in the eye. "Okay, what's up? Trouble at school?"

Andrew shook his head. "Why don't you like me anymore? Did I do something bad? If you stay, I can be good."

Reed felt a pain cut through his heart, and his voice came out gruff and husky. "You're a great kid, Andrew. My leaving doesn't have anything to do with you. We can still be friends and write and talk to each other on the phone."

Andrew shook his head. "It's not the same."

"I know it's not the same, but sometimes people have to split up for a while."

"Like my mom and dad?"

Reed didn't like the comparison, but he didn't know what to say. "Sort of, but that was different, because they were married. We can still be friends."

"Can't you stay? Don't they have enough fires here?"

Reed stared at him, hearing another voice, another time. The day his father had told him he was leaving, he had begged him to stay, promising to help him find the fastest race car in San Diego. But it hadn't worked. And now it was his turn to break someone's heart.

"Andrew?" Jessica's voice cut through the air, and Reed turned to meet her terrified eyes.

"He's okay, Jess. He just got here."

"Thank God." She ran over and hugged Andrew, squeezing him tighter and tighter. The thought of losing her son had panicked her beyond belief. "I was so worried." She pulled back to look at him and then hugged him again.

"Mom, I can't breathe," Andrew complained.

"I'm sorry," she said, laughing and crying at the same time. "I'm so happy you're okay. What are you doing here?"

"I came to see Reed. He didn't say goodbye."

The accusation created a tense silence between the three of them. Finally Reed spoke. "I'm not leaving for a few days, Andrew. I was going to come by and see you." But even as he spoke he wondered if it was the truth. He probably would have just cut and run the way his father had.

"I'm sorry he bothered you," Jessica said stiffly, reading the lie in his eyes.

"He didn't."

"I'll take him home now."

Reed put a hand on her arm, and the touch set off a spark between them so strong that Jessica instinctively jumped back. "Don't," she said.

Reed dropped his hand down to his side. "Maybe we should talk."

"About your leaving? Or about your staying? Because if it's the first, I don't think we have anything to say."

"I care about you both. You have to believe that."

"But not enough to stay."

"It's my career, a chance to move up."

"No, I don't think so. If that was the case, I would encourage you to go. But I think you're afraid of what's happening with us." She paused for a long moment. "I like you, Reed. In fact, I think I could love you, and that isn't easy for me to say, especially knowing that you don't feel the same way."

"What do you want me to say?" Reed asked on an anguished note.

Jessica shook her head in despair. "Nothing that you don't mean, that doesn't come from your heart."

"If you ask me to stay..."

"No, I won't ask you."

Reed took a step back and nodded. "Okay. I'll call and say goodbye to Andrew, if that's all right with you?"

Jessica turned to Andrew, who was still looking sad. "Would you like that, honey?"

Andrew slid off the wall. "Can we go home now?"

"Of course." Jessica put an arm around his shoulders as she led him to the car. She could feel Reed's gaze boring into her back, but she forced herself not to turn around. It was time to go. It was past time.

Reed went home that night feeling like he'd been kicked in the stomach and dragged through the mud. He was a louse, a jerk, a fool. He couldn't think of an adjective that was strong enough to describe his behavior. Worst of all, he was chicken. The stakes were high, and there was more than just his life involved. There were Jess's and Andrew's, too. What if he failed them? There was no answer, so he started packing his things into boxes, preparing to move.

By Sunday morning he had cleared out his apartment. He had put the furniture into storage until he could find a place to live in New York. There was only one thing left to do, take his airline ticket and get on the plane.

"Pancakes are ready," Jessica called out, flipping the last one onto the plate as Andrew walked into the kitchen.

"Can't we have cereal?" Andrew complained.

Jessica sighed, getting a little tired of Andrew's grumpy moods, especially when she felt so much the same. "You've had cereal the last two days. I think a change would be nice." She handed him a plate and then sat down across from him. "Maybe you and I should have a talk."

"Why?"

"Because you're sad, and I think I know how you feel."

Andrew was silent, stabbing pitifully at his pancake, without making any real attempt to eat it.

"I know you miss, Reed," Jessica continued. "But you and I are still together. We're a family and nothing is ever going to break us up."

"Maybe you'll go away, too," Andrew said.

"Never. I will never leave you. I love you very, very much. You're my son. We don't need anybody else, because you and I are a team. If, someday, we find another friend who wants to share our lives, that will be great, but right now, I think we can be happy just being together."

"Why couldn't Reed stay?"

"Because he needs to do something else with his life. But he gave us a lot, didn't he?" She offered him an encouraging smile. "He taught us how to have fun. I don't think we'll ever forget that, and every time we go roller-blading or surfing, we'll remember the good times."

"I just wish he could have stayed."

"So do I, honey."

"I'm not hungry, Mom. Can I go upstairs?"

Jessica looked at his bent head with worried eyes, realizing her pep talk had fallen a little short. "Sure, whatever you want. I'll keep these hot for you."

Andrew shuffled out of the kitchen, and when she got up to cover his plate with foil she heard a terrible banging outside, followed by the sound of someone calling for help.

"Jessica, help me."

Reed? His voice rocketed through her and she ran to the back door and flung it open. What on earth? Reed was standing in the doghouse with the removable top thrown to the side.

"Get this damn dog out of here. He's biting my ankles," Reed complained, hopping up and down as Wiley barked furiously.

Jessica looked at him with one hand to her mouth and then burst out laughing. "What are you doing in there?"

He sent her a sheepish grin. "Since I was in your doghouse figuratively speaking, I thought I might as well get in all the way. Only Wiley is having a fit."

"You're invading his territory."

"Can you help me out?"

"Why don't you just climb out?"

"Because he has his teeth around my pants."

Jessica continued to chuckle as she walked over to him. "That is a pity. Maybe I should call 911. I'm sure the fire department could rescue you. I know they offer very personal attention."

"Don't you dare," he said warningly.

"It's very tempting."

"Just call off your dog."

Jessica walked a little closer until she was standing next to the edge of the doghouse. "Why are you here, Reed? Did you come to say goodbye?"

"No. I came to say hello." He reached into his shirt pocket and pulled out his airline ticket. While she was watching, he ripped it into tiny pieces that fluttered to the ground distracting the dog from his game. "I can't go, Jess. I tried to pretend that it was the best thing, but it's not. I want excitement, adventure and love, and the only place I can find that is here with you."

He put his hands on her shoulders and stared into her eyes. "I love you, Jess, and I love Andrew. I can't run away from that anymore. I want us to be a family." He lowered his head and kissed her until she was breathless.

Dazed, Jessica could do little more than stare up at him. "Are you sure?"

"Positive. I'm ready to make my promises, Jess. You're everything I want in a woman, loving, caring, and a little bit crazy. I've even started to like your buttons." He smiled. "I know it's a risk. We might both get hurt, but I'm going to do my damnedest not to let you or Andrew down. Do you still want me?"

"Are you kidding?" She flung her arms around his neck and hugged him tight. "Of course, I still want you. And as for the risk, I am definitely up to it. I never knew what real love felt like until I met you. I think it's time we stopped thinking about the past or the future. I want to take each day as it comes. I want to watch our love grow stronger, and I know it will. I'm convinced of that."

This time she kissed him, banishing any lingering doubts from his mind. When she pulled away, she smiled at him with promise in her eyes. "Now, if you'd like to get out of my doghouse..."

Wiley barked in reply, and Reed shook his head. "I don't think he's going to let go, and since I am dying to hold you in my arms, there is only one solution."

Reed placed his hands on her waist and effortlessly lifted her over the side of the doghouse until she was squeezed in next to him, his arms wrapped around her body, her face pressed against the curve of his neck.

It was a tight fit with both of them inside and Wiley running around their heels.

"You've probably gotten us both stuck," she complained.

Reed grinned. "I told you the first time we met that I like captive audiences. And now for the show..." He cupped her face with both hands and kissed her with intense longing. With every inch of her body pressed against his, Jessica felt the desire burn deeper between them. She wanted to make love to him completely, without clothes or dogs or children. A laugh slipped out between her lips and Reed smiled against her mouth.

"What's so funny?" he murmured.

"You pick the darnedest places to get close."

"I'm an expert at kissing locations."

"Have you ever heard of a bedroom?"

"Definitely. I've imagined you a hundred times, in a sexy robe..." He plucked at her terry cloth covering, "a little more flimsy than this, a king-size bed and a dead bolt on the bedroom door."

"I think that can be arranged."

"The sooner the better," he murmured, giving her a delicious kiss along the side of her neck.

"Mom, what are you doing?" Andrew yelled.

Jessica smiled at her son's look of amazement, watching the transformation when he saw Reed.

"You're back," Andrew said, hesitating at the edge of the grass. "Did you come to say goodbye?"

"No, I'm staying, buddy, for as long as you and your mother will have me."

His face lit up. "Really, Reed? Do you promise?"

"I promise, Andrew." He looked at Jessica, nestled closely in his arms. "Let's get out so I can hug your son."

He adjusted his body so he could lift Jessica out, but her side scraped against the edge and she wouldn't budge.

Jessica looked at him in disbelief. "We're stuck. You got us stuck in here. I can't believe this."

Reed smiled without regret. "Sorry. But think it of as another adventure."

"What are we going to do?"

"You could kiss me again."

"We have an audience."

"He might as well get used to it."

Andrew clapped his hands. "I know just what to do."

He sprinted back toward the house and Jessica hastily called out for him to stop, but he ignored her.

"He wouldn't . . ." she murmured.

"Maybe he's gone to get a hammer," Reed said. "In the meantime, you and I might as well take advantage of this opportunity."

Jessica laughed. "You're right." With that she grabbed his collar with both hands and planted a long, loving kiss on his lips. It took her a while to realize that the bells she heard were sirens blaring through the neighborhood.

*   *   *   *   *

**Three All-American beauties discover
love comes in all shapes and sizes!**

ALL-AMERICAN SWEETHEARTS

by Laurie Paige

CARA'S BELOVED (#917)—*February*

SALLY'S BEAU (#923)—*March*

VICTORIA'S CONQUEST (#933)—*April*

A lost love, a new love and a hidden one, three
All-American Sweethearts get their men in Paradise Falls,
West Virginia. Only in America...and only
from Silhouette Romance!

Silhouette
R O M A N C E™

SPRING FANCY

Three bachelors, footloose and fancy-free... until now!

Spring into romance with three fabulous fancies by three of Silhouette's hottest authors:

ANNETTE BROADRICK
LASS SMALL
KASEY MICHAELS

When spring fancy strikes, no man is immune!

Look for this exciting new short-story collection in March at your favorite retail outlet.

Only from

where passion lives.

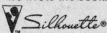

Take 4 bestselling love stories FREE

Plus get a FREE surprise gift!

For all those readers who've been looking for something a little bit different, a little bit spooky, let Silhouette Books take you on a journey to the dark side of love with

If you like your romance mixed with a hint of danger, a taste of something eerie and wild, you'll love Shadows. This new line will send a shiver down your spine and make your heart beat faster. It's full of romance and more—and some of your favorite authors will be featured right from the start. Look for our four launch titles wherever books are sold, because you won't want to miss a single one.

THE LAST CAVALIER—Heather Graham Pozzessere
WHO IS DEBORAH?—Elise Title
STRANGER IN THE MIST—Lee Karr
SWAMP SECRETS—Carla Cassidy

After that, look for two books every month, and prepare to tremble with fear—and passion.

SILHOUETTE SHADOWS, coming your way in March.

SHAD1